You Can't Escape

G·K
Hall
&Co.

Also by Faith Baldwin
in Large Print:

One More Time
A Job for Jenny
For Richer, For Poorer
No Bed of Roses
The Office Wife
Make-Believe
District Nurse
Rehearsal for Love
Beauty
Evening Star
Innocent Bystander
That Man is Mine
The Heart Has Wings
Twenty-Four Hours a Day
Enchanted Oasis

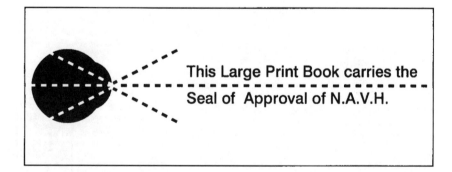

This Large Print Book carries the
Seal of Approval of N.A.V.H.

You Can't Escape

Faith Baldwin 1893-

G.K. Hall & Co.
Thorndike, Maine

Copyright © 1943, by Faith Baldwin Cuthrell

Published in 1998 by arrangement with Harold Ober Associates, Inc.

G.K. Hall Large Print Romance Series.

The text of this Large Print edition is unabridged.
Other aspects of the book may vary from the original edition.

Set in 16 pt. Plantin by Minnie B. Raven.

Printed in the United States on permanent paper.

Library of Congress Cataloging in Publication Data

Baldwin, Faith, 1893–
    You can't escape / by Faith Baldwin.
      p. cm.
    ISBN 0-7838-8408-7 (lg. print : hc : alk. paper)
    1. Large type books. 2. World War, 1939–1945 — Fiction.
  I. Title.
    [PS3505.U97Y68 1998]
    813′.52—dc21
                                        97-48569

You Can't Escape

Chapter 1

October was a blue haze over far hills, and the torches of the trees were burning out in gold and scarlet glory. Benfield, in the westering sunlight of late afternoon, dreamed of the summer just past, of the long, white winter ahead. Gentlemen of leisure, loafing on the bridge at the foot of Main Street, watched the little river running swiftly beneath, full and boisterous after September rains. They pushed their hats back on their heads, yawned, scratched themselves and, re-marking that it was court day, strolled, one and one, or two by two, toward the Courthouse, upstreet, the old red-brick building which housed the jail as well.

Benfield's several church spires, in the manner of New England, soared warningly above the town, pointing a steep way to heaven, and on the Courthouse steps assembled gentry discussed the current session, the recent registration for the draft, the London bombings, Germany's entry into Rumania, and the coming elections, local and national.

They had nothing to do until mailtime, when they would reassemble, properly, at the post office.

There was little traffic on the wide, elm-bordered street. The biggest elm of all was in front of the Courthouse. It had once served as a whipping post.

Now and then cars whipped by, belated tourists returning from the farther mountains, lakes or seashore, hurrying home to rest up after their vacations, to triumph over their frustrated nervous breakdowns and to return to their diverse businesses . . . if any.

South of the main business blocks the Village Green, the ancient Town Hall, the equally ancient Congregational Church also dreamed in the sunlight. There was a warning chill in the air and the blue smoke rose from comfortable chimneys. Way over on West Pond a flock of migrant ducks rose from the ruffled blue surface and flew south in V formation.

The law office of Timothy Wheaton, above the bank, on Main and Elm was very quiet except for the sound of a chattering typewriter. The ample, shabby, but immaculately tidy reception room was empty as a dictator's promise. The door leading to Attorney Wheaton's private office stood open. It revealed a large, uncluttered desk, plain buff walls embellished with framed diplomas, several chairs, most of them uncomfortable, and a great many books. Between the unoccupied private office and the reception room was a small, strictly utilitarian cell, with a desk, a wastebasket, a telephone extension, a straight chair and a window. Also, a girl.

Her name was Linda, and she was twenty-two.

Her hair was the tawny chestnut, sudden with gold and dusky red, which the autumn hills now held, and her eyes were the blue of the autumn heavens; her hands on the typewriter keys, weaving an intricate pattern of whereases and parties of the first part, were good hands, small, strong, tanned. The young man, opening the reception room door and advancing quietly to the threshold of the anteroom, could see her hair and her hands, and the curve of a rosy bronzed cheek, and no more. He could make, however, an excellent guess at her figure. And smiled, with considerable appreciation, because a girl who whistled while she worked, a girl who looked, even at a typewriter desk, happy enough to fly, was a rarity in his experience.

"Hello," he said tentatively.

Linda went on whereasing and whistling.

The young man advanced into the room. He raised his voice. He said, "Hi . . . or am I speaking out of turn?"

The clack of the typewriter ceased. Linda swung around in her chair. Her eyebrows were exclamation points. She said, "I — you startled me," but without reproach.

"I'm sorry," said the young man. He didn't look it. He regarded the small oval face, now in full view. It pleased him. It was — he looked for a word, found one which belonged to another era, discarded it, recovered it again — it was a *sunny* face. The mouth, red as sumac, curved upward, the eyes smiled.

He said, deciding that if and when she stood up she wouldn't come much higher than his shoulder, "My name's Anthony Dennison. I'm looking for Mr. Wheaton."

Linda rose and Tony Dennison suppressed a complacent I-told-you-so. Check. No higher than his shoulder, and beautifully made. The curves went right on, in the right places. There was a nice economy of flesh, not too much, not too little. He observed that she wore a tweed skirt and a sweater. She did them both justice.

She said, "I'm Linda Wheaton. My father's in court . . . but —" she looked at the small, busily ticking clock on her desk — "he should be here any moment now. He usually comes back to the office before going home."

"May I wait?" Mr. Dennison smiled disarmingly. He was a very tall, loose-jointed young man, with a shock of field-mouse-colored hair and pleasant gray eyes. "You see —" He looked around and added hopefully, "If you'll sit down I'll lower myself cautiously to the floor."

Linda flushed. "What am I thinking of?" . . . although she knew of what she was thinking. "Let's go into Father's office," she suggested

She ripped a finished sheet of paper from her typewriter and, with it in her hand, preceded Mr. Dennison into the private office, where she indicated a large leather chair, the one well worn by restless clients who disliked facing the light. She put the sheet of paper on her father's desk and sat down behind it. She said, "You haven't an appointment?"

She looked rather quaint in the desk chair, very small, and unconsciously she had assumed a judicial expression. Mr. Dennison did not bother to suppress his grin. Nice, informal atmosphere about these small-town New England law offices, he decided.

He said, "I'd better explain myself. I'm from out of town . . . and I haven't been arrested for anything . . . yet. Nor am I buying real estate," he added hastily, and was amused by the fleeting look of disappointment which crossed Linda's face. "It's just that I'm driving up to Maine and thought I'd stop off and see your father. My father was a classmate of his at law school — William Dennison."

Linda's face lighted. "Bill Dennison . . . ? I have heard a hundred stories about him —" She opened a cigarette box and offered it to her visitor, with matches and an enormous ash tray. "Father was so fond of your father," she said. "He hadn't seen him in years . . . but . . ."

"Twenty," said Tony Dennison, "the last time my dad was on the East Coast. They met in New York. You hadn't been born then," he guessed, with a rising inflection.

"I was two," she said indignantly. Then her face grew still and grave. She added, "I remember now — your father died, a year or so ago, didn't he?"

"Eighteen months," said Tony Dennison. "He had been ill a long time. I wouldn't wish him back again, if —" He broke off, wondering what deep quality of sympathy and warmth there must be in this girl that he could speak to her as if he had known her a long time. He went on, after a moment, "I'm in a law office in New York. One of those mass production affairs with six partners, three of them junior, and about fifty other lawyers. I'm of the submerged tenth." He smiled again. "And while on my way to do a little camping, a belated vacation, I remembered that your father lived in Benfield . . . the letter he wrote me at the time of my father's death was one I'd not easily forget . . . and so I turned off the main highway and came past, on a chance. I didn't even stop to telephone."

"I'm so glad," cried Linda, "and Father will be . . ."

A voice spoke from the reception room. It was a big voice, as mellow as the autumnal sunlight. It had a carrying quality. "What," it demanded, "goes on here?"

Tony and Linda rose simultaneously, both went toward the door, and collided. Of the two, young Mr. Dennison was the more embarrassed. And Mr. Wheaton asked, surveying them, "Your client, Linda — or mine?"

"Neither," said Tony, before Linda could speak. "A friend, I hope. I'm Anthony Dennison," he added.

Timothy Wheaton's huge hand shot out and enveloped the younger man's. "Bill's boy?" he said. The quick tears came to his eyes. He was like that, tender, boisterous, dramatic, sentimental. Tony remembered a verdict pronounced by his own father, that quiet, forceful man: "Tim Wheaton's of the old school . . . the silver-tongued orator, but one who has a firm foundation upon which to stand, a thorough knowledge of the law and a passion for justice. He would have become a great trial lawyer in any large city. He could have made a national name if he hadn't buried himself in that little backwater town. He has a sense of theater plus integrity and sincerity. You don't often find that combination. He's a big man, in every way."

In every way. Well over six foot tall, and over two hundred pounds heavy. His hair was gray and worn a little longer and much thicker than that of most men. His features were big, craggy, a determined jut of a nose, a bulldog chin, a wide mobile mouth. His eyes were as blue as Linda's.

"Linda," ordered her father, "scat. I want to talk to Anthony. Go home and tell your mother to break out the Spode and Wedgwood, and the Revere coffee pot. Also tell her to see that the spare room fire's lighted. We've an honored guest."

"But look," Tony protested, "I was just . . . I mean I'm on my way to Maine and I thought I'd stop by and say hello —"

"Nonsense," said Tim Wheaton, "you'll stay the night. We've things to talk about. Going to Maine on business?"

"No, camping, but —"

"Driving?"

"Yes."

"Alone?"

"Yes, but —"

"Look here," said Wheaton, "we're wasting time. Sit down. Have a cigar . . . No? Smoke a pipe? Good. Here's some pretty fair tobacco." He reached for a big glass humidor. "Fill her up. And you, Linda, get going." Linda said, "I'll see you both later," smiled and closed the door gently after her.

"Only child," explained her father, "spoiled as the devil. Smart as a whip, though, got out of college when she was twenty, took a secretarial course, and went to work for me. Linda's my staff. Gets paid for it, too," he added, "but not too damned much. There's an office boy and errand runner, George . . . currently, believe it or not, home with the whooping cough. And my young associate, Jud Wilson. Expect to make him my partner one of these days. Good boy, very quick, lacks humor though," he commented, a little sadly, "and, perhaps, heart. Not that those commodities are so highly thought of in these days. He's away, at the Capitol, at the moment. Tell me about yourself," he ended abruptly.

There wasn't much to tell, Tony admitted: Stanford, then law school. After that, his father's office. But his father had become chronically ill and a year before his death young Dennison had come to New York, passed his bar examination there and been admitted to practice. An old friend of his father's had secured the position for him. "You may remember him, Mr. Wheaton: Andrew Powell."

"Class below Bill and me," said Wheaton promptly, "small, dapper, clever . . . now of Ralston, Hammond, Evans and Powell, and Lord knows how many besides. It's a good outfit," he concluded, "but thank God I was never tempted. Too much specialization. Town like this, there's always business . . . little footling cases, according to Powell's standards . . . but a variety of 'em. I get around . . . court of common pleas, probate court, superior court — and the Supreme Court of Errors. Man's cow is stolen, he comes to me. Man's wife is unfaithful, I get the case. Woman's husband throws her downstairs and she comes and sits in that chair and cries a little. I get 'em all, from boundary-line disputes to litigations over wills. Know 'em all too. Half of my clients are my neighbors. The other half drifts in. It's something like being a doctor or a minister. I like it."

"I'm sure you do," said Tony.

"You would too," said Wheaton, "if you'd try it. But no, I suppose you've got New York in your blood. It becomes increasingly difficult to persuade any young professional man to settle down in a small town. Grass looks greener over the fence. Tell me something about your dad, Anthony, and then — where'd you leave your car, by the way?"

"Just outside the office."

"Then I saw it when I came in. Nice little job. We'll talk a bit and then go on home. I always," said Mr. Wheaton firmly, "take a twenty-minute nap before supper."

"But I feel that I'm imposing . . ." began Tony desperately.

"Not a bit of it. Rattle around in the house," said Wheaton, "three of us. Built back in seventeen hundred and ninety, and added to by successive generations. My father had a big family. I was the oldest son — so the house came to me, and a farm too, eleven miles out. But my brother took that off my hands. My father expected me to have a big family. Well, there's only Linda . . . and after the first of next year there'll be just her mother and me . . ."

"She — your daughter is going away?"

"She's going to be married, damn it," explained Wheaton. "You'll meet the boy tonight. Works in the bank downstairs, his father's president . . . owns most of the Main Street business block, and half the outlying farms, and a couple of quarries . . . Rix got out of the university four years ago. He wanted to sell bonds . . . had his eye on Wall Street. We — his dad and I — persuaded him to take it off before he went blind with tears, just looking. But you'll see him for yourself. Meantime, tell me about your father."

It was dusk when they left the office, went down the narrow stairs, and out on the street where lamplight bloomed and made shifting shadows. The leaves were drifting down from the yellowing elms.

Tony's car stood at the curb and Wheaton eased himself in. "Down straight, two blocks, then to your right," he said. "I'll say when."

Tony had driven around the town before coming to the office, stopping at the Corner Tavern to consult a telephone book and ask directions. He recognized, even in the blue dusk, the wide Village Green and the graceful white outline of the Town Hall. They drove around the green and then down a street of old houses set back from the road. Between sidewalk and roadway there was a broad strip of grass and the great trees grew tall and straight.

"White house," grunted Wheaton . . . "as if they all weren't white — on the left. Keep right on in, straight, we'll garage the car."

A few moments later they were walking up the steps of the old, clapboarded house. There were columns, two stories high, and a superb fan-lighted door. The windows of the front rooms went almost to the ground. The house glowed with light and welcome and the door stood open. They went in, Tony carrying his bag, and entered a square paneled hall.

Some time later he was up in the spare room, a little bewildered by the suddenness of this unplanned overnight stop and the warmth of his welcome. Mrs. Wheaton was not much bigger than a sparrow. She was almost as pretty as

Linda, her hair a clear, unfaded red and her eyes a deep, gentle brown. She was quick and brisk and she would not listen to his stammering apologies. She said firmly, "We want you to stay . . . we like young people."

The spare room was huge. A fireplace dominated one wall and a bright fire burned in it, the sound of its burning like the purr of cats. The mantel was beautiful. The four-poster bed was very old and the lowboy and the slipper chair. There were other chairs, fat, comfortable, done in the faded chintz of the curtains. There were bright button chrysanthemums in vases and framed samplers hung on the walls. Beyond there was a small, entirely modern bathroom.

Tony, coat and shirt off, plunging his face in cold water after a quick shave, thought, This is the way to live, after all.

When he went downstairs Wheaton was waiting for him, to draw him into a small, book-filled study, with a battered desk and a glowing fire. A tray stood on the desk, decanter, ice, siphon, glasses, and Wheaton said, "How about it? We've never taken to cocktails in this house. Linda doesn't drink 'em . . . her mother doesn't approve. But a little snort of good whisky never hurt anyone. Let us have one together before Rix barges in. He's coming to dinner and Linda's scraped up another girl — a damned pretty one, by the way — to amuse you. She tells me there's a good movie in town, if you want to ruin your eyesight, after dinner."

They were drinking their Scotch and soda when someone knocked on the door and Wheaton shouted come in and presently Tony Dennison was looking at the handsomest young man he had ever seen in or out of the cinema. Rix Anderson . . . somewhat shorter than Tony — who was six two — but, Tony admitted, without rancor, much better built. Rix was dark and quick, and his features were almost too good. Yet not quite. You forgot the curly, dark hair, the straight nose and sculptured mouth when you saw the laughter in his eyes, the little scar at the corner of the left one, the square chin and strong white teeth, unevenly spaced. You forgave him an almost classic beauty of body, which the dark suit could not disguise, when you felt his handclasp, which was strong and good.

"Rix, this is Anthony Dennison," said Wheaton casually. "Rix is Linda's property . . . or he will be after January third. Grew up together and all that sort of thing. Pretty nice kid," said Rix's father-in-law to be, smiling at him with affection.

He poured a drink for Rix, and the three men stood by the fire and drank. "To Linda," said Rix, with his quick smile.

"Where in time is she?"

"Waiting for Peg, I understand," said Rix.

"Peg," Wheaton explained, "is a newcomer. A charmer. Sets the town by its ears, all the girls hate her except Linda, who can hold her own with anyone, eh, Rix?"

"I'll say," agreed Rix cheerfully.

"Peg and Linda were in college together," Mr. Wheaton went on. "Peg's from your neck of the woods, Tony — San Diego."

"A far cry from San Francisco," said Tony, smiling.

"It's farther from Benfield," said Wheaton. "Anyway, when her mother died — there weren't any other relatives — Linda persuaded her to come up here and open a little dress shop. She's done very well at it. Understand from the women that such a thing was badly needed. She makes buying trips to New York and Boston every so often. She's had some training in a Los Angeles shop, as assistant buyer. Had just a little money, was looking for new fields to conquer, and came to New York first. She got in touch with Linda, came out for a visit, fell in love with Benfield, and has been one of its hard-working citizens for the past year."

He cocked an ear at the door. "Girlish prattle," he murmured. "Shall we join the ladies?"

Chapter 2

If Rix Anderson was the handsomest young man Tony had ever encountered, certainly Peg Reynolds was one of the most beautiful young women. He followed his host into the long drawing room and there she was with Linda; his breath caught in his throat. She wasn't his type . . . that much was definite. Peg was five feet eight, at least. She was as dark as Rix . . . only her hair was the almost incredible blue-black one rarely sees and her skin a rose-flushed olive. She was not merely tanned, as Linda was, her coloring was the same year round, dark, glowing. Her eyes were startling because they were not dark too, they were gray, and very large, under slender black brows. Her mouth was wide, a little sullen, and bright with lipstick. She wore a print dress of some sort, black, with small scattered roses. It fitted almost too well. Her hair was uncut, and worn parted in the middle and knotted at the nape of her neck. It was perfectly straight and smooth and there was a lot of it.

Linda looked like a child beside her, with her short, curly, russet hair and the dirndl frock, clear green, in a sheer wool. Moreover, she looked like a happy child, one who is going to a party and can't wait for it to begin. Then in the course of presentations and small talk Tony saw her eyes go to Rix, he saw her smile at him, and she no longer looked like a child. She looked like a happy woman, secure and proud and humble at one and the same time. It was sweet, it was touching, and Tony found himself a little embarrassed by the way it affected him. He turned and saw Peg Reynolds staring at Linda, as he must have been staring. There was the most curious expression in her eyes. It puzzled him. He thought, Now, what the devil — ?

But it was time for dinner and they went in to sit around the big shining table where conversation was general. Only every now and then Tony would see that expression again in Peg's startling eyes and it worried him because he could not analyze it. You'd say, definitely, hunger . . . a sort of starved, bleak look, and then the next moment you'd say, misery, and finally, defiance . . .

If Linda noticed she gave no sign.

She sat beside Tony, with her mother on his other side, and Rix's good square diamond shone on her small brown hand as she ate and talked. And Tony said, after refusing a third helping, "This is the very best meal I've had in years," and Mrs. Wheaton beamed on him. "Just supper," she said. "Oh, well, dinner, I suppose, but Benfield sticks to the old terms."

Beef and roasted potatoes, homemade pickles and jams, biscuits as light as a contented sigh, golden squash, mashed turnips . . . and along at the end of the meal pumpkin pie and three-year-old American cheddar, and coffee so good that Tony drank three cups.

Her cook, Mrs. Wheaton explained, had been with them since their marriage and the waitress-housemaid as well. They were sisters, and spinsters, and she said, when Ellie was out of the room, "If you think *Ellie's* fat you should see Kitty, in the kitchen!"

After dinner, Linda took a vote. Did they or did they not want to go to the movies? Tony had no wish to go, he saw movies enough at home, but it was a good picture, the last night in town, and none of the others had seen it. So, although they deferred to him and to Mr. Wheaton's, "Look, the boy's driven up from New York and has a long spell to go tomorrow," he voted Aye and was rewarded by Linda's pleasure.

They walked, on Rix's advice. "Otherwise," he said, "we'll be stupefied by surfeit and fall asleep in the most thrilling clinch." Linda, as became the hostess, walked with Tony, Peg and Rix ahead. It was pleasant, Tony thought, walking through the crystal chill of the October night, under a sky blazing with stars, hearing the little wind in the drying leaves, and not too far off the eerie hoot of an owl. Not many cars passed. People walking by spoke to Linda and to Rix. Somewhere a church bell rang for prayer meeting.

"This," he remarked, "is a most lovely town. You're lucky. Or are you and Mr. Anderson planning to leave it?"

"Rix and I? Of course not," said Linda, and laughed, "we'd be miserable anywhere else."

"Your father will miss you in the office," he said, suiting his long stride to her short steps, "Or are you planning to go on working with him?"

"I should say not," Linda said firmly. "You see, I never wanted to work really."

"Why, you lazy little person," he said, amused.

"Oh, work . . . I like it," she explained, confused, "it isn't that. I wanted to take the course and go into the office. It's been fun, as it's a little different from being the usual sort of private secretary. I have to be office manager and bookkeeper as well. I do a lot of odd jobs and I've picked up the language . . . that's a study in itself. I can even soothe weeping or irate clients if Father happens to be out. Sometimes I go into court with him too. No, it isn't that . . . I don't suppose I can make you understand."

"No, you can't," agreed Tony, "and if you hadn't been spoken for I would have tried to coax you to New York. If you wanted a career, well, you could have it there. Good private secretaries who speak legal language, and write it, aren't easy to come by. You have to train 'em. In my firm they're always looking for girls."

"But I don't want a career," she persisted. "I never did."

"What do you want?" he asked her, interested.

"Oh," she answered, "just what I have. Benfield and my own people . . . marriage, and my own home, and a flock of children."

Tony whistled. He said devoutly, "I didn't know that there were any of you left."

"There are lots of us," she said stoutly. "I took the course because Father believes that every girl should be able to support herself. And I've liked working with him and for him. But of course Rix and I have always known . . ."

"Always?" he interrupted.

"Well, I've known since I was ten and he was fourteen," she acknowledged, laughing, "and I think he caught on when he was about seventeen and I was thirteen. It's been that way ever since. We've been formally engaged, if you can call it that since my graduation. But Father didn't want me to marry until I had learned to support myself . . . he has the idea that if anything happened . . . to him or to Rix —" She stopped, as if such a possibility were so incredible she couldn't believe she had said it.

"He's very wise," said Tony.

He felt the entirely natural pang which any young man experiences when, after meeting a pretty girl, he learns that she is quite inaccessible and that someone else has assumed priority. So he said, with the proper amount of melancholy:

"Your Rix is a very fortunate guy."

He thought so again when, after they had returned from the movies, they raided the Wheaton icebox, amply stocked against forays. They had walked home with Peg, who lived a block or so away in the home of one of the town selectmen, and then after the kitchen invasion had been successfully completed — "never thought I'd eat again," remarked Rix, sitting on the edge of the table waving a chicken bone, his laughing eyes on Linda, demure in a pink apron — Tony went on up to bed. He knew better than to stick around when the lingering good nights were being said.

He ascended to the spare room where his pajamas and robe had been neatly laid out on the slipper chair, his slippers beside, and not under, the bed, yawned, smiled, and opened a window. He stood there a moment breathing the cold clarity of the night air, admiring the polished stars, and listening to the sound of a deep-voiced clock, probably in the Town Hall tower, striking the hour. Nice town, nice people. He was sleepy. He had enjoyed his brief stay . . . Linda, pretty girl, sweet, amusing, with a sort of honest naïveté you didn't often encounter these days. Peg Reynolds, well, she was something else again. He hadn't had much conversation with her, of course, but she appeared to be the sort of girl who listened rather than talked, very flattering to the male ego. She was a knockout, he thought, and wondered fleetly why she had interred herself up here rather than taking her chances in a big town where — given the proper contacts — she would slay her tens of thousands.

He heard a murmur below, and leaned from

the screenless window to see Rix and Linda standing together on the steps. He drew back but not before he had seen their embrace, their shadowy figures merging, the long moment of magical surrender.

Tony drew back, feeling embarrassed and a little envious. He hadn't been in love — not really in love — since his senior year in college. What enchantment that episode had held, what disillusion and desperation of grief and rebellion. Looking back, he seemed fantastically young to himself . . . then . . . or else at the moment he felt remarkably old, like Linda's uncle, for instance, or Rix's older brother.

He turned away, sat down on the bed and started to take off his shoes. Footsteps padded to the door, someone knocked and he said, "Come in," amiably. Wheaton appeared, massive in a nightshirt and a tattered dressing gown of sorts.

"Comfortable?"

"Very . . . come in, won't you?"

"Just to say good night . . . and smoke one cigarette. Picture any good?"

"Full of lush, young love," said Tony, "and all that sort of thing. Sure, I enjoyed it."

"I heard you kids in the kitchen and wanted to join you," said Wheaton, "but I was too damned sleepy and besides if I'd come down I would have fried myself an egg or found cheese and crackers and beer. Always gives me colic. The old digestion isn't all it was. We'll be sorry to lose you tomorrow, Anthony. How about stopping back on your way home?"

"Sorry," said Tony, with real regret, "I'm making a wide swing over to the coast, I've promised some friends to stop off. But someday —"

"Someday," said Wheaton heavily. He shook his head. "Seems as if we had to get all we can out of the present," he said mildly, "looks as if we were in for it. A hell of a mess, this world . . . greed and cruelty. What's your feeling on the matter of our getting into the fighting?"

"Oh, we'll get in all right," prophesied Tony. "I had the most curious sensation when I was registering last week. As if it had all happened before. I — I'm so sure we'll get in that I'd like to do something about it, now . . . this minute, and be ready. Several of my friends are flying with the RAF or up in Canada. But, well, I have my mother, you know. She's quite comfortably fixed as it happens, but she isn't well. She's coming east next month to make her home with me — if she can stand the climate."

"I see." Wheaton rose. "Well, I hope you get some sleep. What time do you want breakfast?"

"Would eight be too early?"

"Not in these parts."

Tony went to the bedroom door with his host. They both heard the little clatter of Linda's heels on the old stairway and heard too that as she passed the door she was singing under her breath. Tim Wheaton smiled. There was tenderness and pride in the smile. He said, "She's happy — pray heaven, whatever happens, she'll stay that way."

"Amen," said Tony, "and, of course, she will. Rix seems a fine sort of guy, with all the charm in the world too. Whatever comes, they'll have each other and I imagine, from the little I've seen of her, that she has plenty of courage."

"I believe she has," said Linda's father. "Although it hasn't been tested yet," he added. "She's had a good life, so far . . . popular, friendly — that kid has more friends," he added as if in wonder, "every girl in town runs to her with her troubles, and then Rix. She's been in love with him ever since she was an infant. . . . No," he said, with half a sigh, "she hasn't had to face anything very difficult. We've never had much money but we've always managed to eat and keep this old roof over our heads. We've managed her education too and the absurd things youngsters wear these days, we'll do a bang-up wedding — Rix's father is giving them a little house, an old saltbox, which he owns, two blocks away . . . and there's furniture and to spare in our attic for it. She'll be all right," he added.

"It's very pleasant," said Tony, smiling, "to meet a girl who is perfectly happy. I don't mean in a smug, complacent way . . . but vitally, every inch of her alive with it. And a girl who isn't chasing around after a career. Practically every girl I know in New York wants to be a big shot in whatever she's undertaken . . . business, the arts — you know. Sometimes it's wearing, for a man. I mean, we have to chase too . . . and I've often thought it would be very comfortable to meet some young woman who had no ambitions other than the old-fashioned domestic ones — and who was easy on the eyes as well."

"Linda's like her mother," said Wheaton gently. "And say what you will, modernity and the current unrest notwithstanding, the career of wife and mother is the most satisfactory for any normal woman in the long run. It may not be exciting or glamorous but it has compensations far above front-page headlines and big salary checks. It's biologically sound, for one thing. It endures. It's part of an unending continuity —" he smiled and shook his head — "but don't get me going." He added, "Good night."

Tony shut the door softly after him and went on with his undressing. Swell people, the Wheatons. He'd like to see more of them now that he had found them. Probably he wouldn't. He'd promise himself to run up again, perhaps in the spring, and then, caught up with current obligations and emergencies, he wouldn't. The world moved at too fast a pace these days. You had so little time for the real things, those which counted, as Wheaton had said, in the long run. Yet basically you had no one to blame for this state of affairs but your own harried self.

He snapped out the light, yawned loudly and fell into bed, and was almost instantly asleep.

Linda, next door, heard him yawn, heard him turn over, and smiled. Nice person, Tony Dennison. She wished that he and Peg . . . Of course e, no expression stirred it. Her heart was a welter of emotions. So hard to hate Linda, hard. Linda was a kid, sweet and good and diocre, Linda was just lucky, she'd had every-ng her own way. She hadn't the remotest idea struggle or pain or terror. She knew nothing out loving. She loved everyone, in her frank, nacious way, her parents, Rix, even me, ought Peg, trying to hate her, lashing herself nto it. Linda's a fool — She had no conception f what loving could mean, claws in your breast, earing, bloody, horrible. Linda's life went along on an even emotional keel. She didn't know what it was like to be torn. She'd never know. Nothing would affect her deeply. Her affections were strong, thought Peg, but they remained affec-tions. Not passions, pitiless and compulsory. If anything happened, she would grieve, but she would not be destroyed.

Peg looked up and caught Rix's regard upon her, still and dark, and warning. Oh, Rix, Rix, she thought despairingly, what is to become of us?

He was a coward, she thought, there was no stability under the charm, no promise of strength. It would be easier to hate Rix than to hate Linda.

Someone marched into the long drawing room. The Wheatons' front door was shut against the cold, the sharp wind and snow flurries, but it was not locked. Rix exclaimed from the stepladder and Linda jumped up to cry, "Mother Ander-son."

Rix's mother was a big woman, tall and spare.

she was absurd, as Rix often told her, trying to marry her friends off, just because she herself was so happy, so idiotically, mindlessly happy. She stretched her round tanned arms above her head and sighed, remembering Rix's arms around her in the cool darkness and his mouth against her own and his familiar, "Good night, short, sweet and ridiculous, sleep well."

Of course she would sleep well, in possession of all her little world . . . secure, untroubled. The radio spoke horror and warnings, the headlines were filled with despair and foreboding . . . and Rix had had to register in the draft. But very soon, when the New Year turned, they would be together. Nothing could ever take that away from her. They belonged together, for always.

She thought sleepily that she must ask Tony to come up for a weekend of winter sports . . . she'd have Peg . . . and maybe . . .

Smiling, she fell asleep.

Chapter 3

It was the Sunday before Christmas and less than two weeks before the wedding. "A great confusion," complained Linda's mother thoughtfully. "You don't know which are Christmas or which are wedding presents." She was helping trim the tall tree from the vantage point of a large chair, watching her husband and Rix Anderson toil to string the lights exactly to her taste. Linda was frowning in concentration, hanging the clear, bright globes on the lower branches. Peg, so much taller, had taken over the upper branches and was trimming them with small chimneys and fat Santa Clauses, her dark head on one side. Rix, on a stepladder, sat down on top of it and grinned at them both. "I love to see fragile women work," he remarked.

"You would," said Peg, "you're bone lazy . . . always putting off till tomorrow what should be done today. If we left this tree to you it would be Easter before you had it trimmed."

"Sez you," responded Rix amiably. "You simply don't appreciate me, that's all. Me, I like last-minute action. What's that?" he demanded as Ellie staggered in with an express package.

"Wedding present," said Ellie briefly, "clear from New York."

"How do you know it's weddi   grav
Linda had left her post and w   craz
the big box. She cried, "It's from   so
and that means wedding."   me
"Wait," said her mother, "till I   thi
book."   of
"Rix," said Linda, "help me open   ab
"If I climb down, darling," he pro   te
sonably, "I'll have to climb up again. th
"I'll help you," said Peg.   i
They unwrapped and unwrapped   o
wrapped. The blue box that finally appe t
not very big. But within it, in tissue wr
there was a small and lovely silver bowl.
"Look," shrieked Linda. She took th
from the small envelope. "It's from Ar
Dennison."
"It's lovely," said Peg, turning it in her
red-tipped fingers; "very good taste Mr. D
nison has."
"Rix, you aren't looking."
"Hi ho, Silver," chanted Rix from the ste
ladder. "Do you expect me to clean it, Linda
There's one thing to be said, however. We'l
never go broke. We can always eat the silver,
metaphorically speaking, if we can't eat off it."
Linda sat back on her heels. She wore a dull
wine-red dress in soft wool and a sprig of holly
was caught in her hair. She said, "I'm so sorry
he can't come to our wedding."
She looked up at Rix and smiled and Peg
Reynolds turned away. Her face was still and

Her hair was white and thick and curly. Rix's bright brown eyes were inherited from her, even to the tilt at the corners.

She said, shrugging herself out of her Persian lamb coat, "I was on my way home, but I saw the lights. What time is it?"

"It's nearly five. I'll have Kitty make you a cup of tea," said Mrs. Wheaton, smiling at her oldest and closest friend.

"Do," said Mrs. Anderson, without demur. "I'm half dead. I've been arguing my head off at Red Cross Headquarters. God knows how most of those women ever run a home . . . they're the most disorganized lot I've ever run into. I spend my time cracking the whip." She looked at Peg, and asked abruptly, "How about you, Peg, can't you give us some time, evenings, or does that shop of yours demand your nights as well? Linda's not much use of course. She's walking on clouds —" Alice Anderson's spare brown face softened — "but after the wedding," she added cheerfully, "and the honeymoon, I'll see to it that she does her hand's turn."

Mary Wheaton said, "Linda, run tell Kitty we want tea." She turned to Mrs. Anderson. "The committee on refugees . . ." she began.

"Don't mention committees to me," said Mrs. Anderson, "or I'll scream the house down. Where's Tim?"

"Sleeping off midday dinner."

"So's Horace. *Men!*" said Mrs. Anderson grimly.

"Men must work," said Rix, descending from the stepladder, "and women must weep, over committees." He ruffled his mother's hair with his narrow hand and grinned down at her. "Relax, angel," he suggested.

His mother smiled at him unwillingly. She scolded him, she worried over him and adored him, standing as a buffer between him and his irascible and dour father. But she rarely permitted tenderness to invade her eyes or voice. She had been brought up in a hard, stoical school, it was difficult for her to show emotion, to make the graceful gesture, the gracious remark. She was undisputed leader among the Benfield women. She managed them by sheer steam-roller tactics, a powerful will, a practical mind. She never demanded work that she couldn't or wouldn't do herself and she knew every woman in town, her capacity, her reluctance, or her willingness. She knew those who worked for glory or for what they fancied was social advancement and those who did so because they had to be occupied and those who slaved because it was a principle with them. She knew those who came begging to be put to some use because Anderson was the banker and not just the banker . . . because he owned an enormous amount of property not only in Benfield; because his wife had been born a Hancock and because the Andersons had the biggest house and the most money of anyone in town. The motives didn't matter to Alice Anderson. She might despise them for their motives, she might feel sharp contempt, pity, or understanding but as long as they worked for her, for civic projects, in politics, in charity and church work, she didn't care why.

Linda returned, Ellie arrived with tea and Linda poured. Tim Wheaton came in yawning and disheveled and decided on a whisky and soda and Rix said he'd settle for one too, for sociability. Linda looked at him, thoughtfully — Rix never drank, that is to say the way you meant when you said, "He drinks" — just an occasional drink now and then. But lately . . . She wished he wouldn't. And he had been nervous, crotchety. Twice since — since when? . . . since October . . . wasn't it? . . . they had quarreled. She had spoken to her father about it. You could tell Tim Wheaton anything. She had said, "I don't know what *ails* him."

"Marriage fever," Tim had said consolingly. "Every man gets it. I had such a bad case of it before your mother and I married, Linda, that I damned near ran out on her. Would have too, maybe, only I found out, in time, that she felt the same way."

"How could she?" Linda had demanded. "I — couldn't, ever."

"Maybe not. Maybe girls were a little more scary in those days," said her father, "but men will always be. It's not just the impending loss of freedom, Linda, it's the realization of responsibility . . . oh, and a lot more things. It comes to us all. So you mustn't blame Rix. Walk softly

37

— and don't carry a big stick either. It will come out all right."

Linda thought of this as she watched Rix carry Peg's cup over to her, smile at her and say something under his breath, something silly, because Peg flushed up to her eyes and looked at him, Linda thought, angrily. Funny about them. They were always fighting . . . oh, not seriously of course, yet there was an antagonistic undercurrent. Peg was very critical of Rix, sharp sometimes, almost nasty. Rix took it good-naturedly and came back at her. But it worried Linda. She had asked Rix once, "Don't you *like* Peg, darling?" and he had answered, "Sure I like her, she's a swell gal," and then she had asked Peg, "Why do you pick on Rix all the time, don't you like him?" and Peg had replied, smiling, "Of course I do . . . he isn't my type, especially, but he's all right . . . only not half good enough for you."

She wanted them to like each other. She was fonder of Peg than of any other girl her own age. She'd had something amounting to a crush on her in college . . . and after they had met again, and Peg had been so unsettled and unhappy . . . the loss of her mother, and most of the money, the breaking of her engagement to the boy in the West — Linda had wanted to give her the world to make up, a little, for all she had lost and suffered.

Mrs. Anderson rose and sighed. She said, "Rix, take me home . . . it's sleeting and freezing

38

underfoot . . . I need a strong arm to lean on."

When they had gone Linda sat back and looked at the tree. It was beautiful. She said, "It's the loveliest tree we ever had . . . it will be the happiest Christmas."

"I hope so, dear," said her mother. Her father did not speak but smiled at her. But Peg rose suddenly, so suddenly that she overturned the fragile table beside her, cup and all, and ran out of the room.

Mr. and Mrs. Wheaton raised their eyebrows at each other. But Mrs. Wheaton said gently, "This is a hard season for her, I expect. You'd better go after her, Linda."

Linda fled upstairs. Peg had locked herself in a bathroom. She could hear her, in there, walking about, crying. She hammered at the door. "Please," she said, "please, Peg, let me in."

"No!"

"Please —"

After a long time the door opened. Peg's face was distorted and her gray eyes swollen. She said sullenly, "Oh, Linda, can't you let me alone."

Linda was running cold water in the basin, looking for eyewash, for a cloth . . . for spirits of ammonia. She was a practical little person. She said, "Don't mind me, Peg. I — we all know how hard Christmas must be for you, and you're such an awfully good sport about it."

"I'm a rotten sport," contradicted Peg fiercely. "I hate myself, I loathe everybody. I don't know how you stand me. For two cents, I'd sell out and pack up and get out of this place."

"No, you wouldn't, you just think so now. Business has been good, it will be better."

"It isn't business," said Peg, "it's everything. Sometimes I think I'm going crazy." She came close to Linda, took the cold washcloth from her hands and flung it in the basin. "I'm all right," she said. "No, I don't want aromatics. I don't want anything. I'll go home presently. I'm sorry I made such an idiot of myself."

"You're not going home," said Linda, "you're staying here."

She couldn't bear to think of Peg, upset and unhappy, in the room over at Selectman Smith's. A nice room, and her own bath, and Mrs. Smith was a dear, but it wasn't like being at home. This house should be home to Peg, Linda thought. Aloud she said:

"Don't be a goop, Peg; we want you here whenever you'll come. And after I'm married, I'll have a guest room too."

Peg said, "Oh, be quiet . . . I'm sick of it . . . hearing about the wedding, day in and day out, about everything." She quieted as Linda's face grew stricken and bewildered. "Oh, I'm sorry," she said. She took Linda by the shoulders and shook her. "Haven't you any spirit?" she demanded. "Why don't you kick me out of here?"

"I have plenty of spirit when I need it," said Linda quietly, "but you aren't yourself, Peg. I understand."

"No, you don't," said Peg. "Look, whatever

happens, will you try to remember that I've been grateful . . . and I'll always be sorry?"

"What do you mean?" cried Linda. She was suddenly terrified — alarmed. Peg mustn't go back to that house alone, she mustn't. Linda knew . . . and few others did . . . that after the catastrophe on the Coast Peg had taken too much sleeping medicine. They'd pulled her through that but now . . . she thought, How anyone could do such a thing, life's too precious, too short, too promising . . . But if Peg had once been under that dark urgency — ? She said sharply, "Peg, stop being a fool!"

"Okay," said Peg, and she was smiling. It wasn't a smile you liked. "Okay."

She opened the door and went downstairs and without dramatics made her apologies to Linda's parents. And then, refusing their offer of hospitality or escort, went out alone into the sleet and darkness.

"Golly," breathed Linda, and went back to the living room, "I can't imagine what's wrong with her."

"Nerves," diagnosed her mother, "and memories. After all there was a time when she had everything, Linda — a home, her parents — and now . . ." She shook her head and added, "I hope she'll be all right for the wedding."

Peg was to be maid of honor.

"The wedding," repeated Linda. She sat down on a hassock by the fire and put her hands about her knees. The firelight made sparks in her eyes and red-gold glints in her tumbled hair.

The wedding was very close.

And then it was closer. Christmas had come and gone and it was a week before the wedding. For the last time Linda closed her desk at the office. The girl who was taking her place, whom she had trained for it, would open it in the morning. This was her own week, the week before her wedding . . . there were a thousand last-minute things to do. But she wouldn't get tired, she mustn't. She had seen too many brides fagged out, and hysterical. Rix didn't rate a worn to a shadow and weeping wife . . . he rated the girl who had always loved him, a girl to whom laughter came more easily than tears and whose heart held a deep and abiding awareness of peace and content, under all the surface disturbances of wondering and wishing, of excitement and expectancy.

She went home, walking through the cold darkness, with the snow in her face. Her father had gone to the county seat, for overnight. Her mother would be out, she had some calls to make and might be late. Linda went into the quiet house, grateful for its warmth, for the smell of something baking, for the firelight.

She was taking off her things when the telephone rang and Ellie hurried out of the kitchen. "I'll take it," said Linda.

A voice she did not recognize spoke to her; it asked, "Linda . . . ?"

"Yes . . . Who . . . ?" but now she knew. Rix's mother. She must have a cold, she was so hoarse. Linda said, "Mother Anderson, I didn't know you at first. Have you a cold? You mustn't have a cold, just before the wedding."

Alice Anderson said, painfully, "Is your father there . . . or your mother?"

"No." Linda explained their absence. Then her voice sharpened with sudden anxiety, "What's happened? Is anything wrong?"

"I hoped," said Mrs. Anderson dully, "that Mary or Timothy —" she broke off. "Is there any place I can reach your mother?" she asked.

Linda's heart constricted with unreasoning terror. She said, "I don't think so, she told me she had some calls to make . . . she didn't tell me where. Mother Anderson —" she took a deep breath — "has anything happened to Rix?" she managed to ask.

There was a silence which seemed very long. Then Mrs. Anderson said, "Linda, I'm coming over . . . I'll be there as soon as I can."

"But has anything —"

The wire was dead.

Waiting was interminable, waiting was an eternity. Linda walked from the door to a window, from a window to the fireplace. Something had happened to Rix.

An accident.

He had driven to Boston on the previous day, on business for the bank. He filled several positions in the bank. He was his father's confidential secretary, over and above anything Miss McFaddin did. He was in the Trust Department. He was often in Boston on business. He was, he said, a glorified errand boy.

An accident. The slippery roads, the blinding snow flurries, the long run. Rix drove too fast. He always had.

Rix. Rix.

People didn't wring their hands in real life. Linda had always thought that, reading about it. Yes, they did. She was wringing hers now. They were cold and wet. Her stomach turned over. She felt ill, with waiting.

Oh, God, no, don't let it be anything like that. Don't You see, can't You understand, it's just a week before the wedding?

Perhaps he wasn't badly hurt. Just a minor accident, after all. Peg would tell her she was crazy to feel like this, to anticipate trouble, to dwell on death when it might be a scratch, a broken leg —

You can postpone a wedding.

She was back at the fireplace staring into the flames, seeing only Rix, dark, laughing. Rix, on the golf links, swearing at a sliced ball. Rix, dancing at the little club, his arms tight around her. Rix, at college, the year he graduated. Rix at high school, playing football. Rix . . .

She heard the step on the porch, and stumbled toward the hall. Alice Anderson came in, shaking the snow from her coat. She *looked* like death.

She walked like an old woman.

"Linda . . ."

Mrs. Anderson's arms were around her. "Don't cry," she said. Linda wasn't aware that she was crying. "Linda . . . I'd rather die than tell you this . . . that a son . . . that my son . . ."

Like death, her face, white and stern, and old. And Linda crying, "What is it, what has happened to him?"

"He's gone," said Mrs. Anderson, "with Peg Reynolds. She met him in Boston. They've gone on to New York, they are to be married there. I had a wire. He asked me to tell you. Linda . . ." Her harsh voice broke. "Oh, my child," she said pitifully, "don't look like that, don't shake so —"

"I don't believe it," said Linda, in a loud, bewildered voice.

"It's true," said Mrs. Anderson. She released the girl and went toward a chair, groping as if she were blind.

"It is true," she said again.

Chapter 4

Long afterward Linda realized that for a considerable time she was too stunned, too incredibly shattered, to touch the match of decent anger to the untidy rubbish of her emotions and let them burn up in a clear hot flame, cleansing and solacing. The nightmare quality of the days and nights following Rix's elopement with Peg Reynolds persisted but it was as if she dreamed this fantastic thing through a veil, as if she could not clearly see the figures struggling against the background of the dream. She was predominantly conscious of a sense of complete emptiness . . . no, not complete. For there was a core of hard, implacable suffering, but everything else was hollow and uninhabited.

It was she who had consoled Rix's mother, instead of the other way about. Alice Anderson had received a shock from which she would never quite recover. She was wholly honest, a woman of high standards and personal integrity. Rix was her only child. She loved him beyond anything in the world. If there had been times when she admitted his weaknesses to herself, his too easy charm which permitted him to slide over difficult situations as oil over water, she measured this against his many endearing characteristics —

46

amiability, humor, and a definite gay tenderness and sympathy. She could not understand the dishonesty, basic in his repudiation of Linda, as she had always been convinced that his was a compassionate heart and that he would not willingly hurt any other human being. But it was now borne in upon her that his long habit of sliding away from the unpleasant had here asserted itself. He had been utterly incapable of coming to Linda and of saying, I thought I loved you. I find that I do not . . . I am in love with Peg Reynolds and she with me. And so I must ask you to release me from a promise, which if kept would bring only unhappiness, not alone to me and to Peg, but to you.

Whatever compulsion had drawn him and bound him to Peg it was more potent than the familiar conventions, the standards of his household, the rule of thumb by which his parents lived. It was quite natural that Mrs. Anderson, although she did not seek to excuse him to Linda or to Linda's parents, nor even to his own father, believed, in the privacy of her heart, that the whole affair was Peg's fault . . . that she was the stronger, in being weak, that she had used the unfair weapons which lie in every beautiful woman's hand.

Whether Mrs. Anderson was right or wrong made no difference.

Rix's father walked with an additional stoop. Never a particularly genial man, he was just, honorable, a little austere. New Englanders like their bankers thus. They have an instinctive distrust of too obvious cordiality, or backslapping and easy good-fellowship. They like a hard bargain, and admire a man who exacts the last legal percentage. For if he was too freehanded, too easy with the bank's money, what would become of your own?

He said simply that he would have nothing to do with his son or the woman he married. He was through. If ever a crown prince, an heir apparent had abdicated a throne, Rix had done so. His great-grandfather, his grandfather, and his father had built up their position through hard work, vigilance, and an unrelenting sense of honor. This Rix had destroyed in one cruel, unconsidered action. Rix had, Mr. Anderson reminded his wife, a small income of his own, enough to feed him and Peg, and to keep a roof over their heads. He was not brilliant but he was clever enough, he would be able to get work. She need not fear that they would starve. But as far as his father was concerned, his hands were clean washed of the boy.

He was fair about it. It was not what Rix had done but the manner in which he had done it. Had he been honest, had he said that he found he no longer loved Linda Wheaton as a man should love the woman he intends to marry, it would have been a disappointment to his father and a lasting regret. But not a blow, such as this was. He said heavily, "You can't tell me this is sudden . . . it must have been going on for some time." There was only one right time in which it could have been settled, and that was in the beginning. Even if Rix hadn't been sure at first that it *was* Peg and not Linda, if he had wavered from Linda to the extent of not being sure, then was the time to break the engagement . . . or rather to ask her to abrogate it. But to sneak away, to plan this devious route of escape, to send a wire, leaving the difficult explanation to be made by his mother — that was the rub. He couldn't be honest. He couldn't face an issue. There was nothing of the surgeon in Rix, he dared not make the clean cut . . . painful, of course, but capable of healing because it was clean.

So Anderson said to Tim Wheaton, "There is nothing I can do, Timothy. If I could apologize for Rix, but that's no good. I can say that I am sufficiently ashamed of my son to regret that I fathered him. That too is not enough."

He came to see Linda. It cost him a great deal to walk heavily up the steps, take her hands in his, and look into her pinched face. She had lost her summer patina of bronze during the winter months. Now she was quite colorless, even her mouth, under the bravery of lipstick. He said merely, "There's nothing I can say," and she was startled to see tears in his small, direct eyes. She could find it in her heart to be sorry for him, for both of Rix's parents. She said quietly, "It's all right, Father Anderson." It would be hard to grow away from the special terms of intimacy;

49

she could, she supposed, return to Uncle and Aunt, which as a child she had called them.

Her own parents broke her heart, if it was capable of breaking again . . . and indeed it was, day in, day out. It's a pity hearts do not break once and for all. Mary Wheaton was utterly bewildered. On that cold, blowing evening when she had returned to her home to find Linda white and very quiet and Alice Anderson distracted and in tears, something very close to her sense of security had been threatened. They had had such a good life, she and Tim and their daughter . . . a life which would go on, its continuity unbroken, in Linda and her husband and children. Now everything was changed, and unstable. She experienced, toward morning, an utterly alien fit of wild and rebellious anger, alone with Timothy in their big room. She had managed to get Linda to sleep. It had taken the assistance of Dr. Elbron, the old, blustering, reliable man who had delivered her of Linda and had watched over the child ever since. He had come plodding up the slippery steps and into the house and met her in the hall. "She doesn't want you, Mac," she said pitifully, "but I can't get her to sleep . . . and she won't cry."

"What's it all about?"

Sooner or later he'd hear, so she told him now, briefly.

He spoke his mind in a few precise words. They were not words which Mary Wheaton normally liked hearing but she liked to hear them now. They said something for her. He added, pulling himself up the stairs by the banisters, "She'll have to cry."

Linda lay in the big bed in her room. It was a room Mac Elbron knew by heart. Here she had lain as a baby, here as a child, here as a growing girl. He had seen her here, flushed and incoherent with scarlet fever; mildly ill with measles; sick to her bones with influenza. Here he had talked to her seriously and gently, supplementing the information her mother had given her when she was approaching adolescence.

Old Mac sat down and said, "This isn't a very pleasant state of affairs, Linda."

She did not answer.

He said strongly, "Forget it, forget him, forget them both. They're no good. You've more to live for than Rix Anderson. Pull yourself together. You've a lot of fight in you, pride too, and courage. He wasn't worth loving. Now that you know that, you can go on from there."

They'd treated her very tenderly, her parents and Rix's. It was as if she were a person who had been so badly battered and bruised that they dared not handle her lest they inflict another hurt or set her wounds to bleeding, and her nerves to the consciousness of too much pain. But not Dr. Mac.

He made her cry, finally, sat beside her for a time and afterward reached for the glass of water Mary Wheaton set at his hand and took the tablets from his battered medicine case and

51

forced them between Linda's lips.

He did not leave until she was quiet. He went out of the room, leaving Mary there, and spoke to Tim Wheaton in the hall. "She'll do," he said, "and she'll get some sleep. Don't try to make it too easy for her, Tim. It's like an ulcer. It may heal over the top, but that's no good. It has to heal from the bottom, slowly, soundly. Don't treat her as if she were made of glass. There's too good stuff in that kid to go to waste. You can't let her waste herself. Put her to work. None of this I'll-take-her-on-a-long-trip-to-forget business, even if you could afford the time or spare Mary for it. She won't forget that way. She'll have to forget from within herself." He paused. "The hell of it is," he added, "I liked that boy. I thought they'd be happy and that I'd — Well, it doesn't matter now. Sure, he was always a little weak. Alice has spoiled him, although she doesn't know it. Being weak isn't too dangerous if what character you've got is sound. I thought Rix was like that. I thought Linda had strength enough for two, in her way. It's a way you don't find often among youngsters her age."

After Linda slept Mary Wheaton returned to her room to find Tim smoking by the window, in his shirt sleeves. The old pipe, the one he loved best, the one he always smoked when things were wrong, as if the familiar grain of the bowl was comfort, in his hand, the warmth and smoothness.

He had knocked it out and taken her in his

arms and let her cry and when she had stopped he had listened to her outburst of anger. She said all there was to say and he nodded. He said slowly:

"I'd like to beat him within an inch of his life. But what good would that do anyone, Mary? There's not a damned thing we *can* do but try to pick up the pieces and fit them back together. I don't know if we can even do that. Maybe it's just up to Linda. God help her," he petitioned, low.

It was no ordinary thing, you see, he told himself. Not just a case of girl meets boy, falls in love and then something smashes it up. She'd loved him before she fell in love with him and when she fell in love with him finally, she went on loving him too. There's a difference there. Rix was her world. Oh, we rate, her mother and I, we're her world too, but in a different way. All her dreaming, all her illusions, all her hope of long happiness were centered in Rix Anderson. And she isn't the type to recover easily, to find substitutes.

Linda woke. Waking was dreadful. Waking out of the drugged dreams, with a heavy head and a lagging consciousness . . . waking to blink at the cold winter sunlight and the sound of chickadees at the feeding box in the tree outside the window . . . waking to wonder, before full awareness returned, *Why* do I feel like this, what has happened? She was so used to waking strong, free,

feeling the rush of vitality, and the sure knowledge that this was another day, a good day, a
wonderful day, one day closer to the wedding.

Wedding.

She didn't cry. She was numb, and the cold
crept from her feet and slowly upward to her
heart, upward to her lips, until she shook with
it, the nervous chill she could not control. Get
up, go through the everyday routine, go down to
breakfast, face this thing, there are a hundred
things to do, a thousand . . .

Why did you do this to me?

She wasn't sorry for herself. She was sorry for
Rix's parents and for her own. Not for herself.
She hadn't room for self-pity and she did not
want anyone else's pity. She had told Peg
Reynolds, some time ago, that she had plenty of
spirit. All right, where was it?

She had told Peg . . .

Funny thing, you lose your love and you lose
your friend and then you know that they never
really existed. Rix was never my love, she
thought, or this could not have happened. Peg
was never my friend.

Linda rose, and her head ached unbearably.
The floor was unfriendly to her bare feet, and
she went on shivering . . . a hot bath, so hot she
could hardly bear it, might help.

She thought, I'll go to the office, and then
remembered that she was through at the office,
another girl had taken her place there, one who
needed the work. Linda recalled that she had

worried for months because she felt she was taking a salary which didn't belong to her, which would be vital to someone else.

Her father was alone at the breakfast table. As she slid into her place beside him and Ellie, composed but with her eyeballs reddened, came with fresh coffee and a barely discernible grimace of greeting, he said, "I'm letting your mother sleep."

The sun poured in, the plants bloomed on the stand by the window and Mary's canary almost burst its golden throat with singing. The sun shone on glass and silver, on honey in a crystal dish, on marmalade in another. The room smelled of flowers, air and sun, of coffee and bacon. Linda's eyes narrowed against the light. Her head throbbed. Her stomach tightened against the odor of food. She felt ill. She asked Ellie, almost inaudibly, for dry toast. She poured her coffee, black.

Wheaton cleared his throat when Ellie had gone. He said, "Your mother had a pretty bad night. She's taking this pretty hard."

A faint flicker of astonishment, almost resentment, stirred in Linda's eyes as he had hoped it would. Her mother was taking it hard, she thought. Why should she? She had held her love for more than Linda's years, she would have him until one of them died . . . perhaps afterward. Her mother's life was full, not empty.

He added, "It is always hard for her when you're hurt."

Linda was silent. After a time she said, "She needn't worry about me."

"That's pride," said her father, "isn't it? And a damned good thing too. It's first aid, and emergency treatment. It's not the ultimate treatment, Linda. But it will serve you, if you'll let it . . . and don't let it master you instead." He looked at her and she raised her eyes from her empty plate. He had aged, she saw with detachment. He said, "We're in this together. We'd like to help you, we will, to our fullest capacity. But the person who will help you most is yourself. You know that, I think."

She said, "Yes, I suppose so."

Ellie came in with the toast, set it down and went back to report to Kitty in the kitchen that it would break your heart to see her sitting there, white as a sheet and her eyes like burnt holes in a blanket and not eating a bite.

"If I could get my hands on him," said Kitty darkly and surveyed her hands, which were large and very capable for all the cushioning fat.

"All right," said Tim Wheaton to his daughter. "You aren't going to let this beat you. Not for long. And there's no use my telling you you're well out of it."

"None at all," she said evenly.

"I thought as much. You'll learn that the hard way, I suppose," he said, "if ever."

There was silence. He thought, looking at her, that hearts literally bled. His did, drop by drop. He remembered the time Linda had scarlet fever and hadn't known him, remote in her delirium. He remembered old Mac saying, "It's touch and go, Tim." He remembered the way he'd felt then. This was something like it. This was history repeating itself. You sat by and watched your kid suffer and there was nothing on God's earth you could do for her. That time long ago Mac had fought for her, armed with medical science. Neither could be of any avail here. Medicine hadn't progressed to that degree. No use to say, Time will do it, Linda, time. What was time to a youngster who was trying to reconcile the long past with the longer future and the brief, horrifying present?

He said abruptly, "You're the doctor." He didn't have to add, Physician, heal thyself.

Ellie came in with Mary Wheaton's tray and Linda said, rising, "I'll take it up."

Ellie hesitated and Tim Wheaton frowned at her. She surrendered the tray reluctantly and went back to the kitchen to report to Kitty: "Her hands were shaking so I was scared . . . but she carried the tray out of the room and her back as straight as an arrow."

At the door Linda paused to look over her shoulder at her father. She believed that he couldn't realize what this simple action must cost her — mount the stairs, knock at the door, go in and face your mother's grieving eyes, set the tray down.

She said, "I'd rather you'd try not to be so sorry for me."

Chapter 5

Life was simple — and also complicated — in Benfield. There was a weekly newspaper and an item could appear in it only after the event: ". . . the engagement . . . has been broken by mutual consent." But that would hardly make sense with Rix already married, would it? Let it go . . . no item.

Also practically everyone in Benfield knew Linda Wheaton and Richard Anderson — Rix to them, because that was how he had termed himself as a very small boy and the name clung. All young people of his age and Linda's had gone to grade and high school with them. Their parents were friends, neighbors, acquaintances . . . Or at least knew them by sight. *There's Linda Wheaton . . . doesn't she look awful?*

Mary Wheaton went about her committee work and Alice Anderson about hers. If murmurs stopped when they entered a room they gave no sign. Now and then a man spoke to their banker or lawyer fumblingly. "Sorry to hear," they'd begin, clear their throats and go on about their pressing business, a mortgage, a loan, an overdraft, a boundary dispute, a divorce, a will.

Linda had a great many friends. Most of them sincerely loved her. They were very kind. The few closest to her — but not so close as Peg had become . . . and some of them remembered that — spoke to her openly enough and she listened and thanked them. They called her up, asked her to parties, asked her to do this and that. And the men she knew, those who were still in town, drifted back, the telephone rang . . . would she go to the square dance at the Town Hall, would she go to the movies, would she take in the basketball game?

She would and she did, setting her chin, controlling her hands, laughing when it was expected of her, trying to listen, making by some miracle the right answers.

She told her father, "I'd like to go back to the office but of course I couldn't, now Eva's there, and she's satisfactory."

"Not as satisfactory as you were."

"But she'll learn; and it wouldn't be fair."

"No, it wouldn't be." He hesitated, that evening, sitting by the study fire, and asked, "How about looking for another job?"

Linda shrugged and shook her head. She was still pretty white. Rix — and Peg — had been gone a month. She had lost weight. Her little bones showed.

"Not here." She leaned forward, looking into the flames. "I — I can't stand it here."

"Nonsense," said Tim Wheaton, and felt like weeping.

"I've tried, terribly hard. Everyone — knows. Oh, it isn't that, it isn't that sort of pride. I

59

can't explain. Everyone's sorry for me. But some of them look at me as if — as if they were asking themselves what was wrong with me. Why couldn't I hold what I had, what did I lack that Rix . . . ?"

He interrupted. "I see. Don't tear yourself to pieces like this, Linda."

She said after a moment as if she hadn't heard, "I've got to get away. There's nothing for me here."

There you had it. Twenty-two years of love and devotion, twenty-two years of caring for her. They didn't count. There was nothing for her here because she had fallen in love with a boy and he'd run off and married someone else. Well, take it, that's what parents are for, I suppose, take it and like it or, if you don't like it, keep your mouth shut.

He asked, "What do you want to do?"

"I don't know. I think, go away by myself, and work. In New York . . . I remember Tony Dennison said he could get me a job with his firm . . . I had a letter from him —" She broke off.

Tony hadn't said anything about a job in the letter. He had written because she had returned the silver bowl. She remembered the silver bowl because it had come when they were trimming the tree and Peg had helped her open it, and Rix had sat on top of the stepladder and refused to come down to gloat over it and had been absurd about cleaning silver.

All the wedding presents had been returned . . . with little notes. They hadn't been easy to write. Because everyone knew why. Tony Dennison hadn't known why. The letter to him had been somewhat simpler. Just that you weren't going to marry Rix, after all. He might be one of the very few who would think, ". . . the engagement . . . broken by mutual consent . . ."

Her father said, "All right if that's the way you want it. We'll miss you, Linda. But New York isn't very far away, even I get there now and then. And perhaps you're wise."

"Perhaps I'm not," she said, "perhaps the right thing to do is to live right here, find some sort of job and face it, and go on seeing the same people day and night, and . . . but I just don't seem to have the guts."

"I'm glad your mother didn't hear that," he said, and smiled faintly; "it isn't one of her favorite words."

"It's a good word," Linda said, "and it means something good, if you have it. I haven't. I don't like the person I'm becoming. Sensitive, neurotic, imagining all sorts of crazy things, shrinking — inside me, I mean — from the most common-place remarks, from things people say, without meaning anything. I can't live with myself. I went to the movies last night with Fred Diston . . ."

"Nice boy," commented her father, "used to be a heller, but grew up pretty steady for all his red hair . . . took over his father's business as if he were born to it."

He thought, Fred used to be crazy about her. One nail drives out another, they say, but I don't think Fred's the man — or the nail.

She went on. "He asked me to marry him, you know, about three years ago. Not that he didn't know how I felt about Rix. I don't know why he bothered. Last night, coming home from the movies, he didn't say anything but he kissed me. I let him. It's nice to know you're wanted even if there isn't anything in you that responds. Afterwards I told him I was sorry. It wasn't any good, even the knowing. And then after I was home I wasn't as sure about the knowing. I thought, maybe he didn't . . . I mean, maybe he was just sorry for me, or maybe he figured . . ." She broke off helplessly. "There's no use not facing it. I was always so confident . . . so sure . . . of people, of myself. That's over. I feel insecure. I feel afraid. I think if I were with people who didn't know me, in a place I didn't know, a place in which I'd never lived, it would be different. New York was always just a holiday place to me, a picnic ground. I went there with you and Mother or to visit, for amusement, for pleasure. It wasn't my place. I don't know more than half a dozen people there, so if I went there to live and *made* it my place . . ."

She was quiet and he waited. She said after a moment, and he was startled and disturbed by the adult gravity of her face, and the curious remote look in her eyes, "I could make good, I think. I'd work, because it would be all I had.

Working, before, was different. It was something I did because it pleased you, you wanted me to do it. I liked it too, it was fun. But it was marking time. It wasn't even as much as a means to an end. I did it well because I don't do things halfway but still I did it as other girls knit or sew or make watercolor sketches. There wasn't an ounce of me in it," she explained. "I was just waiting. I suppose there are thousands of girls like me, who don't give a whoop for the job beyond wanting to do it decently and be worth their pay. They want other things. I did. I thought I had them . . . or would. Well, that's washed up. This time I want a job, without favors and where I'm not known. Something I can get my teeth into, and which will come to mean more to me than anything else because it will be all I have . . . and," she ended, "maybe all I want."

"I see," said her father painfully.

She said slowly, "I'm afraid Mother won't be happy about it."

"If it will make you happy, she will be."

She looked at him, almost in anger. "Don't you understand, I'm not looking for happiness? What is it, anyway — something you dream up all by yourself, something you create? I don't know. I want to be busy," she told him, almost fiercely, "I want to be occupied, and so tired at the end of the day that I can't think or feel. If good times come along with it, that's all right too. The kind of good times that don't matter, they're a change, that's all, from what you're

63

doing, and you can forget about them."

He asked after a minute, "Shall I write Tony Dennison?"

"No," she said. "I'll call him after I get there, if I don't lose my nerve. I've my own money as a backlog," she reminded her father.

It wasn't much. Her grandmother had left it to her. It was in a savings account. Her father and mother had never had to ask her to draw on it, for clothing or education. It was all hers. And she had said to Rix, laughing a little, drawing his arm around her, holding it close, "And you can't have it either . . . nor the house . . . no one can . . . except our first baby. It's going to belong to him. It's going to set him up in business sometime, or buy him a ring for his girl when he gets himself seriously engaged." And Rix had said, "Maybe he will be a girl," and she had answered, "So much the better, you've no idea the silly uses to which girls can put money."

Her father said, "Don't bother about it. We'll see you through."

"I'd rather you didn't," Linda said. "I — I'd like to be on my own."

She had hurt him rather badly. She knew it instantly and put her hand on his knee and then withdrew it. One of the tragic things, to him and to her mother, was the loss of the spontaneous gesture of affection, as if she were afraid, as if tenderness and its expression alarmed her, as if she must hold herself in an upright position or go to pieces.

"I'd always come to you if I needed anything," she promised him.

He rose, and said, "All right, Linda. It must be nearly dinnertime. I'll talk to your mother first if you'd rather but it would be kinder, I think, if you told her yourself. It will be natural for her to be upset — at first. She may find it hard to understand why you wish to go away from the people who most love you. But in the end she'll see. You must do" — his voice was a little unsteady but he controlled it — "what you believe best."

"Yes," said Linda uncompromisingly.

He reflected, as he watched her leave the room, that nowadays the sunlight touched but could not reach her. A fanciful thought, he told himself, exasperated. You sentimental old fool, he added. But always Linda had carried the warmth and light of her own sunshine wherever she went, into whatever room contained her small and vital person. Not now. Curious, inexplicable, how a young woman could change, in so short a time. Perhaps all change is growth. I wouldn't know, he thought. It wasn't that she seemed hard or bitter; merely that the warmth had gone. If Rix had died, he told himself, even her bereavement would not have altered that special quality which had seemed integral to her.

Linda left for New York late in February. She had arranged to live in a clubhouse for young businesswomen. It wasn't what she wanted, but it had to do. In the first place, the comparatively modest rental was all she could afford; in the second place, her decision appeared to comfort her mother. At least she would be with other people, girls of her own age, and would have a friend close by, as the sister of one of her class-mates, whom she knew slightly, was manager of the club. "Of course," she wrote Linda, "we have a house mother who is a precious antique and should be kept under glass. She's supposed to take over when one of the inmates of this insti-tution has a cold in the head, a difficulty at home, or a dud love affair. I keep the books and operate on the practical side. I'll be awfully glad to see you, Linda. You knew Sally was married? I miss her a lot."

On the way to New York, Linda thought that at least neither Sally nor her older sister, Cynthia, would know about Rix. She and Sally had never been very close and Linda had met Cynthia Warren only when she had come up to college to see the younger girl.

The Andersons had been at the Wheaton house the night before, to say good-bye and to refrain from saying the things so obviously on their minds and hearts. But Alice Anderson had managed to draw Linda aside. She said, too completely Rix's mother just then, to spare Linda:

"Linda, if you should see Rix . . ."

"I don't expect to see him, Aunt Alice."

"I know . . . but sometimes things just happen.

He writes, and I answer, although his father isn't happy about it. He — they — have an apartment and he's taken some sort of job in a brokerage house." No, she couldn't say, See him, write me how he really is, how he looks, if he is happy. She shook her head and tried to smile. "Forgive me," she said, with unusual humility.

Well, Linda was on her way, her way out — taking the road which led away from memory, from the knowledge of other people's knowledge, from pity and discussion and speculation. She would be free of all that, free to make her own life. It wasn't the life she had wanted or planned but it would have to do and it would be the best life she could make.

Her trousseau went with her. That might have been funny, she reflected, if she could see anything amusing in it. But on the practical side she couldn't afford to give away the things she had bought — for Rix . . . the colors he had liked best, the fashions he had found becoming to her. She couldn't afford a whole new trousseau — for a career, this time, not for a marriage — but she could, and must, afford a whole new life.

She reached New York in the bitter black dusk of the cold winter night. The cold was damp and went through your clothes and ate into your very marrow; it was not like the dry, exhilarating cold of Benfield. She gave her bags into the care of a redcap and taxied to the club, which was uptown, on the West Side. Cynthia was there, expecting her, and it was, after all, pleasant to be made welcome.

The club was a big, red-and-white brick structure, and Cynthia a lean, tailored young woman of thirty with a plain, humorous face. She greeted Linda warmly. "And your cell's waiting for you. Dinner's over, by the way, but I've wangled coffee and sandwiches. I didn't know if you'd have anything on the train."

"I should have stopped in the station," Linda said; "the train didn't have a diner, as it happened."

"Well, let's get you settled first," said Cynthia briskly, "and then we'll invade the kitchen. I have certain privileges, and God knows I should, on the starvation stipend they pay me." But she didn't look starved, no matter how thin. She added, "You'll meet Mrs. Fitzgerald later. Let's go. You'll be glad to know we have all the luxuries, a self-operating elevator for one, a roof — which is not practical for sun bathing at this season, and a pool. If you hadn't decided to room alone we might have found better quarters for you. But as it is, I've changed you from the original room I marked on the plan to a corner — the only single corner room, with shower. It's within what you said you could pay and you are lucky to get it. The gal who had it suddenly lost her mind and eloped."

In the elevator Cynthia remarked that perhaps after Linda had been there a while she might change her mind about board. The club served breakfast cafeteria style, and dinner "complete with waitresses." On Sundays there was a combination breakfast-lunch. "The food isn't too bad," said Cynthia, walking down the corridor while William, the club's errand boy, trailed along with the bags, "but it gets monotonous."

On their way to Linda's room various heads, blond, red, brunette, popped out of doors and hailed Cynthia. "One big happy family," Cynthia explained, unlocking Linda's door. "The friendships that spring up! And the hates . . . and the feuds. It's wonderful!"

The room was all right. It had two windows, and was bright with bearable chintz. There was a good reading lamp, a small desk, a bureau, an excellent mirror. The tiny bathroom was adequate. "This is one of the best chairs in the house," said Cynthia, sitting down by the window. "And the closet isn't too discouraging. You can unpack your trunk when it comes, and store it in the basement."

I wish she'd go, thought Linda.

"Have you a job yet?" asked Cynthia.

"No, but I hope I'll have one soon," said Linda, with a confidence which at the moment she did not feel.

Cynthia rose. "Well, wash your face and hands and trot down for your coffee and meet Mrs. Fitz. Don't be misled by her resemblance to Whistler's mother. And don't tell her too much. Take a tip from one who knows. Fitz leads a vicarious life, made up of all the events large and small which occur to the club members. She'll give you lots of advice. Ignore it."

The door shut, and she had gone. Linda sat down on the edge of the bed and looked around her. She saw only her own room at home, and Rix's picture laughing at her from the wall. She heard her father's heavy step, her mother's voice, and Kitty and Ellie arguing in the kitchen. She could feel the lovely wood of the banisters under her hand, she could smell the atmosphere of the Wheaton house . . . it smelled of wood smoke, and tobacco, of cookies baking, of pine boughs and flowers and fresh air. It was the very odor of home. Her throat tightened and her eyelids burned. She found herself saying aloud and absurdly, "If I were a man I'd go out and get drunk."

When she finally went downstairs Cynthia was waiting for her in the small office off the central hall. "And here, my child," she explained, "is the lounge where you are permitted to entertain young men until eleven P.M. Never, never in your room. Not many young men are entertained here, however, in any sense of the word, as they immediately experience the sensation of being in a zoo. Rut they light here briefly to wait uneasily for the appearance of the girl friend, after which they grasp her firmly by the arm and rush her out into the night. The rules are simple enough. If out, you are supposed to be in by midnight. If for some reason or other you can't be, you notify Mrs. Fitz before you depart. If you go away for a weekend you are supposed to sign out with address and telephone number so that the club may reach you if there's news from home. You may smoke in your room. That is a recent condescension. And here is the dining room, and here the kitchen. This," she added, "is Olga, who looks after the inner man. Olga, this is Miss Wheaton for whom I commandeered the coffee and sandwiches."

Olga was amiable enough and Linda drank the coffee and ate a sandwich at the kitchen table. She asked Cynthia about Sally and sat listening to a sprightly description of a little gray home in the west, complete with two dogs, a cat and a new husband, hardly hearing. Once Cynthia broke off to say, "I thought . . . didn't Sally tell me that you were engaged?"

Well, everyone in her class at college had known that much, everyone within her orbit.

Linda shook her head. "It's all off."

"I see," said Cynthia; "well, better luck next time." She grinned, and added, "You've come to the right place." She looked at Linda critically. "You're very pretty," she commented, "though you could do with a little flesh on your bones and some color. I thought girls from your neck of the woods were bursting with sunkissed health. However, it won't be long before you acquire the city robustness and a little research will acquaint you with those refugees from a wolf pack with whom every gal comes in contact — even those who look like Dracula's daughter."

They left the kitchen and went into the lounge, where presently Mrs. Fitzgerald joined them. She was a small woman, in respectable black, with touches of white lace and a multitude of beads. She had a pink and white face, not much lined, and mild blue eyes. She was of the type which, as Tim Wheaton would put it, ran over at the mouth. Linda murmured, "You are very kind," so often that she felt like a worn-out phonograph record. "You must look upon me," urged Mrs. Fitz, "as your mother by proxy. I mother all my girls."

Cynthia provided the escape. She mentioned the fact that Linda must be tired, and went with her to the elevator and up to her room. She said, lingering at the door, "You won't sleep well, the first night. None of 'em do. But you'll get used to it . . . and after a week not even the most vociferous taxi horn will bother you."

When she had gone Linda unpacked her night things, wrote a note to her mother and went to bed. She lay in darkness and wished herself at home. But she wouldn't go back. Not until she had proved to herself that she could make herself over, not until she ceased to mind the trivial, hurting things . . . eyes which remembered, the pity of indignation in friendly voices.

She thought, Tomorrow I'll telephone Anthony Dennison.

Linda woke, and lay for a time adjusting herself to her surroundings, to the unfamiliar noises beyond her door, the chattering and laughter as people passed on their way to breakfast. She got out of bed and went to the door on the inside of which the meal hours were posted. She would have to hurry. She had lain awake so long that when, finally, she slept it had been with the sodden heaviness of fatigue.

Into the shower and out of it, the tweed suit in which she had traveled, the silk blouse and oxfords. She brushed her shining hair and reddened her lips. Outside, in the corridor, girls spoke to her, introduced themselves. "You're new here, aren't you?" they'd say. And downstairs Cynthia waited for her.

"Here's your tray. This is a catch-as-catch-can affair," Cynthia told her. "I've saved a table for us. You'll have plenty of time to catch up with the names, ambitions, and frustrations of all our members."

But several members stopped at the table and there were the necessary introductions. Pretty girls and plain young women and others not so young, girls who had jobs or had recently lost them, girls recently in from out of town, looking for work, girls working by day and studying by night.

"Why," suggested Cynthia, "don't you take the day off and get yourself turned around? I'm free this afternoon and evening. I'd be glad to take you under my slightly frayed wing."

Linda smiled. She said, "I'd like that, very much. But I must try to get an appointment, first."

"The phone booths are in the hall," said Cynthia. "When you've made your plans, let me know."

Cynthia was a good person. Linda liked her. It was instinctive, she could not help it. She had liked her when she met her at college. Don't like her too much, she told herself, never like anyone too much again.

That was the way it had to be: you lost love, you lost friendship, you were betrayed. Never as long as you lived must you put yourself in such a position again, one in which you could be hurt. Once was enough. It must not happen twice. Like people, with reservations. People were useful, she thought, as long as you didn't let them get under your skin. You could have fun, if you stayed on the surface. If you made up your mind that you could grow an armor against confidence, against intimacy, you would be all right. You'd get along better — more safely.

Sometime later when she thought he might be in his office, she looked up Anthony Dennison's firm and telephoned him. She was a little while getting through to him. When she did he was delighted.

"Linda Wheaton," he said, "what are you doing in town?"

She said, "If you must know, I'm job hunting. I haven't any right to inflict myself upon you but —"

He said, "Get yourself down here . . . wait a minute . . . make it about twelve-thirty, will you?

74

We'll have a talk and then I'll feed you. It will be swell seeing you."

Leaving the telephone booth she ran into Cynthia. "You look pretty smug," said Cynthia, regarding her. "Get a bite?"

"A nibble or the beginning of one. I've an appointment. Twelve-thirty and for lunch . . . I don't know how long I'll be," Linda added.

"Call me," said Cynthia. "If you haven't called before three I'll know you're tied up." She put her capable hand on Linda's shoulder. "Good luck," she said.

Tony Dennison was just as Linda remembered him, sitting across the desk in the office he shared with two young lawyers, both of whom were absent when Linda arrived. He said heartily, "You look fine. How are your dad and your mother?"

They were well, she said.

He said, "My mother's here with me now . . . I told you, didn't I, that I expected her? She runs my apartment, and my life, for me. You must have dinner with us soon." He leaned back in his chair and his eyes sobered. He said, "I was sorry to learn from your letter that your engagement had been broken, but then I wrote you that."

That's what he thought. Wonderful to be with someone who thought that. Cynthia too. Linda said evenly:

"It's all right, Mr. Dennison; best thing all around."

75

"Must we be formal?" he inquired, an eyebrow raised. He added, "You might have kept the silver bowl. It was for you, you know."

She said, "I couldn't, naturally," and smiled to soften that. She added, "I wonder if . . . do you think there's a chance for me here?"

"I wouldn't be surprised," he said cautiously. "We'll talk about things over a luncheon table. You mustn't mind the place I'll take you to. It's noisy but near and the food is good. Afterward, I want you to meet the woman who handles our stenographic and secretarial personnel, Miss Covert. She's something of a Tartar but you'd get on with her."

At luncheon Linda told him where she was living. She added that if she got the job she contemplated a night course in law.

"You?" said Tony, staring at her. "But . . ." He shook his head. He added sadly, "Good Lord, you've changed."

"Perhaps," said Linda.

"You don't really want to be a lawyer, do you?" he persisted. "I can't imagine, that is . . ."

"Not particularly," she said. "I mean I haven't any special desire to pass bar examinations and go into practice. But the more I learn the more chance I'll have in, for instance, your office."

He was still shaking his head. He said, "Well, more power to you, but you've picked a pretty stiff schedule for yourself. Better see how things go at the office first."

"If I get the job."

"Oh, you'll get it," he prophesied blithely. "We need bright gals. I've already spoken to Miss Covert. But I wanted to keep you dangling for a little. We'll go back there after lunch and make the fatal arrangements. I wish," he added, "you were going to be my secretary. But my office has one already and couldn't dislodge her with a pickax. I'm afraid they'll assign you to one of the higher-ups."

They were walking back to the office when he said, too casually, "By the way, funny thing, I ran into Rix Anderson the other day . . . A gal I know threw a party, and he was there and — and —"

"Peg," said Linda as quietly as she could.

"Sure," said Tony, with evident relief. "She — they were looking very well," he said inanely.

"That's good," Linda told him. She thought, ashamed and desolate. So, after all, he knows.

She said aloud, sturdily, "I didn't explain, in my note. I didn't think it would matter, or that you'd ever know. But if you have seen them, then you do, of course. I mean, someone must have told you — your hostess perhaps. She'd say, 'This is Rix and Peg Anderson . . . they're bride and groom.' "

Tony was considerably embarrassed. Linda did not look at him but she could sense it in his voice, as if his voice blushed. He said, clearing his throat, "Sure, something of the sort."

"I don't suppose it matters," said Linda, after a moment, "but it wouldn't be difficult to go a step further and discover just *when* they were married — which was a week before . . ."

She stopped and swallowed. Tony thought, Poor kid. He thought, What the devil's wrong with Rix Anderson . . . as if this youngster isn't worth six of that beautiful —

How would he feel, he wondered, if his girl ditched him shortly before a contemplated marriage? Not that Nelda Heron was his girl yet . . . but because he had suddenly fallen in love, not so long ago, he felt very tender toward Linda Wheaton whose man had fallen out of love with her.

"Don't let it throw you," he advised uneasily. "I —"

She said, "If I wanted to, I could tell you that I broke it off and that Rix turned around and married Peg out of pique. But you wouldn't believe that, would you, after seeing them together? And I won't let it throw me, Tony. You'll see. You get me the job and watch my smoke. That's all I want . . . a job and a chance to work at it, with everything in me. And if you dare feel sorry for me —"

He said gently, "I'm a hell of a lot sorrier for Anderson, who didn't know his luck."

Chapter 6

The Wall Street offices of Ralston, Hammond, Evans and Powell looked out over water and up into sky. The building which housed them soared fantastically high into heaven. And the atmosphere which surrounded them was upper income bracket, and therefore often equally blue.

These were offices with dignity, a certain restrained charm and a soothing quality. When the elevator discharged you in the corridor and you were faced with the closed doors, glittering with names, you might know a moment's hesitation, but once you had entered the reception room hesitation fled. You had come, you knew, to the right place, and the right people for consolation, reparation, advice . . .

The reception room had large comfortable chairs, the lighting, whether natural or artificial, was always correctly subdued, there were multitudinous ash trays and plentiful magazines, all of current issue. The female receptionist had the dignity that would discourage lounging at her desk, with its battery of telephones, but she was also very pleasing to the eye — in order that, from a purely artistic and visual standpoint, you might not regret a longish wait.

These offices dealt in the law, which presupposes justice. They were equipped to handle your case, my case, anyone's case . . . provided it was of comparative importance. You did not approach Ralston, Hammond, Evans and Powell if you owned a two-family house and your tenant refused to pay the rent. But if you owned a couple of apartment houses, in the right district, and any difficulty resulted which your own management and legal department could not conquer, then you came here and consulted with the proper authorities.

Ralston, Hammond, Evans and Powell drew wills, were often named executors, arranged for divorces and separations, managed the minor multiple legal difficulties of many lucrative clients, represented seller, buyer, or lessee of large blocks of real estate, and was famous for its knowledge of corporation law. . . . The particular department of the firm dealing with corporation law was very large. But the impressive firm name did not tell the current story, as Mr. Ralston had long since retired to a 3,000-acre farm in Virginia where he raised horses and wrote his autobiography, and Mr. Hammond had died two years ago.

Linda Wheaton looked at the calendar on her desk. It informed her that the month was now May and the date well along. She had entered the firm's employ on the Monday following her introduction to Miss Covert and had served a sort of roving apprenticeship as the firm had long employed the now-familiar Washington method of maintaining a stenographic pool. The partners and the junior partners — whose several names did not appear in gold letters on the outer door — had their own secretaries, tried and true. But there were half a hundred young lawyers, neither senior nor junior partners, who toiled within the firm and they needed secretarial services. Likewise, *mirabile dictu,* there was a night shift. "The real reward," Tony once told Linda, "of being married to a legal light, however obscure, in this outfit is that if your husband says he has to work at night you can check on him by picking up a telephone. There's always someone there to answer it."

Late in March Mr. Powell's secretary became ill. Linda was therefore sent to the Powell office, an impressive dugout, merging all the better aspects of a costly mausoleum, Grand Central Terminal and the Public Library, as a substitute during Miss Peters's first absence, which lasted a week. Andrew Powell was just as her father had described him, small, dapper, very charming and exceptionally clever. She had performed her duties satisfactorily for some days when, upon a rare occasion, Mr. Powell was not in consultation or busy on the long distance telephone and he bethought himself to ask her graciously about herself. She told him, with some reservations which did not include the suppression of her father's name. Linda had wisely decided that to force herself upon the attention of her father's college

81

mate would not be cricket . . . but if the proper opportunity arose, she saw no reason why the information need be withheld.

Mr. Powell was enchanted. He observed Linda with more than the usual mechanically pleasant masculine reaction to her undeniable attraction and when Miss Peters returned to her job he arranged matters so that Linda could be installed as secretary to one Mr. Thomas Yorke, a junior partner in the trial division of the firm, a personable young gentleman with all the instincts — when not too occupied — of the well-bred wolf.

Linda was no Little Red Riding Hood. She conducted herself with propriety if no priggishness. Tony, who knew Mr. Yorke too well, emitted an occasional warning. She was seeing something of Tony. He had fulfilled his promise to present her to his mother. Linda had dined at the Dennison apartment a number of times, and Tony took her to lunch now and then when he was free. "Do you think it proper?" she had inquired, and he had replied, "As I am not even a junior partner no one can accuse me — or you — of office politics. Besides, we're old friends."

They both experienced their promotions, so to speak, at about the same time. First Miss Peters resigned, on a pension, and Mr. Powell commandeered Linda's services. She was perfectly qualified. She had worked for her father long enough to be versed in at least the broader outlines of such a job, and likewise had served an apprenticeship in the firm, with a fling in the Powell office itself. Also, as none of the other experienced firm secretaries were in a position to be shuffled around like a deck of cards, it was fortunate that Linda was at hand. No girl need be hauled up from the general pool and specially trained, no one new to the firm's methods need come in from outside.

Then, a week or so later, Tony Dennison was made a junior partner. This event had been in the offing for some time and thus did not come as a surprise, but called, nevertheless, for a celebration. Tony was, as it happened, the youngest man in the firm's employ to receive such an honor — which, on the material side, meant an excellent salary, augmented at the end of the firm's fiscal year by the partnership cut . . . the percentages achieved by so junior a partner were not stupendous by any means, yet they represented a considerable additional sum. In order to achieve his new position Tony had had to prove himself, first of all, a damned good lawyer and, second, one capable of bringing paying clients into the firm. This he had done: three of the newer, excellent accounts were due to his efforts.

In modest recognition of his own success, Tony gave a dinner . . . and Linda attended. Mr. Yorke also was there, and a number of other young men, most of them connected with the firm. Tony's charming, fragile mother was hostess and there were a number of pretty girls, among them Miss Nelda Heron, whose father,

Walford Heron, of the Heron Manufacturing Company, was Tony's latest triumphant personal client, the final wedge to junior partnership.

Nelda, Linda perceived, was blond, beautiful and played the field. She also perceived that the new junior partner was almost embarrassingly smitten. With the new detachment with which she now observed other people's emotions, she wished him well and hoped he would not get hurt. She was, moreover, rather glad of this situation. For if you yourself have forsworn love and lovers, you can regard the spectacle of a man in love with someone else with friendly interest and no envy. It makes a nice basis for friendship.

On this May morning, after looking at the calendar, Linda went into Mr. Powell's office with the opened mail. He was not present, having departed for Washington. A number of the letters she could attend to, herself. The rest must await his return. Mr. Powell had several appointments which she must tactfully postpone as the Washington trip had been undertaken on very short notice. She had also several small personal duties to perform for her absent employer, theater tickets for Mrs. Powell, an allowance check to send to the Powell heir in Princeton, and there was also the matter of the rather difficult letter to the Dean with which Mr. Powell had entrusted her. She would compose the first draft, and it would await his approval, revision and signature.

Linda looked critically at the large polished desk, spotless, its austerity softened by a vase of spring flowers but not by Mrs. Powell's silver-framed photograph. Mr. Powell's wife was on the formidable side.

She was back in her own anteroom, having just completed the last of her telephone calls, when Tony burst in. He said, "Hi, where's his Nibs?" and Linda told him.

Tony raised his eyebrows. "I've heard rumors . . . well, if he goes to Washington and you go with him, what shall I do? I find the mere thought unendurable. Have you heard from your mother? It was swell to see her and your dad last week. And that reminds me, how'd you like a weekend in the country?"

"Are you propositioning me?" asked Linda coldly.

Tony looked at her and reflected a little sadly that it was not the sort of thing Linda Wheaton would have said back last October. He regarded the well-cut black dress, the autumn-leaf hair, short, sculptured to her small head, the subdued but effective lipstick, and reflected further that she had changed in a number of ways. She had become standardized; in speech, in dress, in general appearance, in — reactions. Last October she had interested and charmed him through her effortless vitality, her warmth, and the inner happiness that glowed through her as flame through crystal. Now the vitality was leashed to her job, there was little warmth, and if she was happy she made no parade of it. He asked suddenly, gravely:

"Linda, are you happy?"

"The grasshopper mind," said Linda severely. Relenting, she smiled at him, her eyes very blue and direct. "Of course. Far happier than I deserve. Father told me I was shot with luck . . . and he's right. It was too absurd, ushering him into Mr. Powell's presence, on a formal call. I didn't want him to make an appearance, naturally. It looked a little like a veiled, if cordial threat . . . you take good care of my only daughter — or else. But it didn't turn out that way at all. I could hear them laughing in there like kids and smell pipe smoke — father's pipe, of course. And then they went out to lunch and Mr. Powell telephoned I'd have to postpone his first afternoon appointment . . ."

Tony frowned. He did not seem to be listening. He walked over to the window and regarded the flawless view. Over his shoulder he said, "And about that weekend?"

"You haven't told me anything about it."

"Nelda will. She'll telephone you tonight, at the club. She's pretty tired with all these charity affairs, relief work and what not, so she's pulling out of town on Friday afternoon, late. She wants you and me to drive up with her, and Thomas Yorke. The Herons have a place in Connecticut —"

"That fact hasn't escaped me," said Linda.

Tony turned back, grinning. "It has been rather publicized," he admitted, "but after all, when you've that much money what else is there

to do with it? The yacht's laid up — retrench-
ment fever on the old gentleman's part — and
they've closed the place at Southampton and the
Palm Beach shack. So there's nothing left but
the Connecticut place and the town triplex."

Linda, considering, said, "I don't know . . .
I'd feel a little out of place, I think."

Tony glared at her. He said, "Back in Benfield
you weren't a snob," and she gaped at him in
astonishment.

He added, more gently, "Don't be a goon,
Linda. Nelda likes you, she took a great fancy to
you the night of my dinner." He grinned a little
and added, "I must say she had every reason to,
as you were very helpful."

"Just because Tom Yorke got fried to the hat,"
said Linda, "and you —"

"Not quite to the hat," argued Tony. "And I
hadn't been since back in the old university days.
Not to that extent, anyway."

She said, "Well, as long as your mother understood I thought Nelda should."

"You were swell," he said gratefully. "Nelda
thought so too. She complains that you never
give her a break, you turn down all her invitations . . ."

"Not quite all of them," said Linda. "I did go
to that cocktail thing one Sunday . . . the week
you were in Chicago. Never saw so many people
in my life. But you know yourself I haven't time
to lunch socially, and can't work on any of her
committees, and certainly can't pub crawl and

be on the job next day. Besides, I can't possibly repay her, and I don't like being under obligation."

He said coaxingly, "Well, pocket your stern and rockbound pride for once and come along on this weekend shindig. I don't really believe Tom's particularly serious about her — or anyone else. I noticed you diverted him very nicely the night of the dinner. So take him on, Linda, there's a good girl, and give me a clear field for once."

"Well," she said, sighing, "I'll consider it. The country would be fun."

"Horses if you want to ride, all that sort of thing," he said vaguely. "Swimming pool. It's heated . . . so, if the weather's good . . . Anyway, she'll call you tonight."

"I'll see," said Linda. "By the way, why aren't you in court?"

"We got a stay," he told her. He went to the door, turned and grinned. "Did you know that your mother and mine had begun a beautiful friendship?" he inquired. "A big box arrived yesterday from the Wheaton pantry — beach plum jam, apple jelly, mustard pickles, wild strawberry preserves . . ."

"She told me she was going to send them," said Linda.

When he had gone she went about her routine duties, with the careful, intelligent precision which Mr. Powell expected of her. She coped with a difficult and worried client (female) by telephone and a difficult and belligerent client (male) in person. She found certain files which Mr. Evans's secretary required for Mr. Evans. She talked to Mr. Powell on the long-distance telephone and took various instructions which had just occurred to him. She canceled tomorrow's luncheon appointment for him, and looked over the draft of a speech he was to deliver before a Bar Association dinner later in the week. She informed Mrs. Powell that the theater tickets would arrive at the house by messenger in the afternoon . . .

And all the time she was thinking that it was May in Benfield, it was spring, and she not there to see it . . . the reluctant spring of New England, delicate, lovely, capricious.

Homesickness was a disease, it was an infection. She had battled it all these weeks and months. She thought she had conquered it but now and then it attacked her again, in the whisper of wind against her cheek, in the frail shadows of new leaves, in the spilled yellow of forsythia in the parks and the first of the fruit blossoms. Her parents' trip to New York had come as a complete surprise to her, they had notified her only just before they left Benfield. "Business," her father said, but she knew better than that. His business was to see her, to find out for himself how she was looking, how behaving. They came to town, stopped at one of the bigger hotels, took her to dinner, and returned to the club to see her room for themselves and to meet

Cynthia, to whom they took an enormous fancy. Mrs. Fitz was not so successful and Tim Wheaton's very eyebrows disapproved of her despite his courtesy. But Mrs. Wheaton professed herself as satisfied with her child's surroundings.

During their stay they dined, with Linda, at the Dennisons', they took Cynthia and Linda to a theater, and Tim Wheaton called upon his confrere, Mr. Powell. They left on a Sunday night, so Linda had all that day with them. She went with them to the train and it was while they were standing at the gates with so much left unsaid that Mary Wheaton put her hand on Linda's arm. She said, "Aunt Alice sent her love . . ." And as Tim turned away to speak to the gateman she added, low, "You — haven't seen Rix, have you?"

No, she had not seen him. So far as she knew no one had, no one known to her, except Tony . . . long ago at some dinner party or other. He had never mentioned Rix or Peg or the occasion since.

Her mother said, sighing, "Alice worries. He doesn't write often . . . he realizes his father's attitude. Peg has never written."

Linda asked, in a hard little voice, "Did you expect that she would?"

"No, I suppose not . . . it seems such a pity," said her mother, and then Tim turned and the porter beckoned and the business of having their tickets checked at the long desk was over and they had gone.

They had urged her to plan a vacation during the coming summer, and to return home, but she wasn't going to ask for one. She didn't rate one, she said, and thought secretly that she would rather stay here. Not rather; she must. She couldn't at this stage permit herself to become softened by familiar surroundings and the old way of life. It was too soon, too soon.

She had not gone to night school. Tony had dissuaded her, and later her father, writing from home. "It's too big a load to carry just yet," he advised. "If you are serious about it nothing would please me more. I'd like you to take your course, pass your bar examinations and be admitted to practice, in your own state, in my office. But don't bite off more than you can chew, Linda. Not now, anyway. Get settled, give yourself a year at least, familiarize yourself with the organization of a big law office and then make up your mind. There's no use rushing into things . . ." because, he thought, but did not write, you've been so hurt that your only idea is to kill yourself with work — kill your memories and your emotions . . . as many hours of the twenty-four as you can spare from sleep.

Walking to the subway in the late afternoon Linda smelled the spring in Manhattan, dusty and disguised by the odors of humanity and automobiles . . . but nevertheless perceptible. Look down the narrow streets to the west and see the golden rose of sunset, and look up at the sky, feel the little wind on your cheek. Lilac time, flower time, blossom time . . . even in New York you know it, it's in your blood and your bones. You have seen a lot of springs, Linda, but never so strange a one as this, in a city of steel and cement, in a city where you are still a stranger . . .

The dusk was blue when she reached the club; the spring dusk and the lights piercing through it, the lamps of the park blooming into yellow flowering. Across the wide ocean the lamps had gone out, as a man once said of another wartime. Misery and fear, destruction and hunger, blood and courage and, she thought, I walk in the dusk and want to cry because it is spring again and Rix isn't part of it, not for me, not any more, not ever. I'm small and petty and a fool, but there it is.

Even in war you have to be young, you have to be hurt, you have to think of things which affect you, they are more real to you, after all. People die, the bombs fall . . . and still you have to think of Rix as you walk up the club steps and ring the bell.

When she felt like this, lonely and egotistical, selfish and unhappy, she hated the club and the friendly people, the girls who wanted to swear eternal friendship, the smell and sound of the crowded dining room, the inevitable talk of dates and jobs, bosses, injustices and men. She hated the very sight of Mrs. Fitz in her decent black asking, "Have you heard from home lately?" She even wished that Cynthia were not so kind. Cynthia, who had learned — or who had always known how — to accept only what was offered and to offer only what was acceptable.

She thought, If Nelda calls me, I'll accept the invitation. At least I'll be getting away from the club! Perhaps, too, a little away from myself. Nelda's pleasant. I'm fond of Tony and Tom's fun — in a way. It will be a change. I could do with one.

Chapter 7

Tony called for her on Friday evening. Nelda's plans had altered several times during the week, and Linda thought, as each change was daily reported to her, You'd think that a girl who looks as she does would have a tidy mind! However, the final arrangements were that Nelda, and a young married couple who were to chaperon the weekend, would go up ahead, on Friday morning. "Because if not," Nelda told Linda tragically over the telephone, "I'll be roped into that awful cocktail party Friday afternoon . . . it's a war relief affair and sometimes I think if I see another refugee in diamond stomacher — I suppose cocktails are their form of relief — I'll scream!"

Linda, therefore, left the office at her usual time, went to the club to change her clothes and do her last-minute pressing and packing. Cynthia, wandering up to her floor, knocked, came in, and sat on the bed watching her. "How," asked Linda, distracted, "do people dress for weekends in Connecticut when they say, Don't dress, bring old clothes, and in the next breath tell you that any simple little long frock will do?"

She surveyed her suitcase; slacks with which she could wear the sweater she had on under her tweed suit. The suit jacket was all right over the slacks. Her oxfords would do country duty. A crepe wool dress, full skirted; a shirtwaist dinner dress, long skirted and sleeved. Slippers, a change of shoes, her housecoat. She sat back on her heels and surveyed lingerie and stockings. She said, frowning, "They ride and all that. I don't, so I don't have to worry about riding clothes — which I don't possess. As for swimming —"

"Who ever heard of swimming in May in this climate?" inquired Cynthia.

"Their pool's heated," said Linda absently; "besides, it's always hot around Decoration Day."

Cynthia thought, She certainly has a lot of clothes. She reflected further that the lingerie Linda was packing had evidently not been taken out of its tissue wrappings before. There was a lot of it in the bureau drawers which now stood open. These were the sort of things of which the average girl had a few, for evening, for best, when she came to New York job hunting. But these looked . . . these were, she saw, monogrammed. She thought, suddenly, They must be trousseau. So it had gone that far. I wonder what happened and why? She said nothing as, in the few weeks Linda had lived at the club, Cynthia had learned that she was not prone to bestow confidences. A curious thing, because, when Cynthia had first met her, during Linda's senior year, she had seemed such an open, direct little person.

Linda got up, closed the suitcase, closed the bureau drawers. "Well," she said, "they'll have to do. I've put in a couple of thin blouses."

"What's she like?" asked Cynthia, suddenly.

"Who? Oh, Nelda Heron? Very beautiful," said Linda critically, "in a lean blond way which just escapes being haggard. It's diet, I suppose, or glands, or something. I think she was meant to be on the Juno type; her mother is, a very impressive woman, handsome, with lots of façade, if you know what I mean. But Nelda's like a squirt of Vichy. She has beautiful hair, which she's never cut — that is, it's shoulder length — and there are interesting hollows under her cheekbones. Tony said she was Glamour Girl Number One the year of her debut. That was some time ago, I suppose, she's about twenty now, maybe twenty-one. I don't know. But they come out early here, don't they?"

"Very early. Cradle to Stork Club. The other way round would be more appropriate, I think," said Cynthia, laughing.

Linda looked in the mirror, remade her mouth, ran a comb through her hair. "Now that I'm going," she said, "I wish I weren't."

Silly, she reflected, they'll all be strangers except Tony and Tom, no one knows about me except Tony and I don't mind him knowing — much.

Tony arrived in a small car, and indolent William took Linda's bag downstairs and she followed. They drove out of the city along the green parkways, and turned off the Merritt at Norwalk to have dinner at the Inn on the Silvermine River.

"We'll take the back roads from now on," said Tony; "it's slower, but more fun. I told Nelda that it would be foolish to plan dinner at Heroncrest."

"What!"

"Absurd, isn't it?" he agreed blandly. "But that's what they call it. I didn't know if I'd be held up at the last minute. As you know — or should, if a few months with our sainted firm has taught you anything."

With sunset it had turned cool, and was not quite warm enough to eat outdoors, and in one of the big fireplaces logs snapped pleasantly. They had a cocktail in the small lounge, and Linda admired the figure of the demure woman standing at the bar . . . in direct defiance of the old Connecticut laws. She was life size and the bartender had placed something that looked like an authentic drink close to her hand. The big rooms were hung with the unlikely portraits of bygone generations, cadaverous children and grim family groups. A thousand relics of other years decorated walls and rafters, ancient inn signs, wooden pestles, innumerable bits of hardware, the outlived usefulness of which was hard to fathom.

Between cocktail and dinner they went out on an unroofed porch, the trees growing up around it, and looked at the little river below them, widening into placidity, the trees leaning down from either bank. The stars shone down in the magical dusk, which was not quite night, and swans floated on the surface, as effortless as dreaming, close to the edge of the little dam over which the river fell with a soft rushing of waters to the rocks below.

"It's lovely," said Linda, "and so peaceful."

Tony said, "It's a funny thing. I knew Mr. Heron, of course . . . I met him early last summer at Piping Rock. I was out there with some friends. That's how the whole business started, and very good too. Later, although I was at his house innumerable times, I still hadn't met Nelda. She was usually off somewhere. Then one Sunday, oh, shortly after I was in Benfield, he drove me up here for luncheon. She was in the car. Afterward we went on to Heroncrest for the afternoon. The place is never closed, there are always caretakers there, but the reinforcements, so to speak, had all been moved back to town, by then."

Linda thought, He'll always love it here because this is where he first knew her. She wondered just when he had fallen in love with Nelda. She thought, miserably, that there was no special place with which she associated Rix Anderson, except all of Benfield. Not that they hadn't had their favorite haunts for lunching and dancing and dining. The Crag, for instance, high in the mountains . . . a sprawling, precariously perched log cabin, with great fires and wonderful food, and in summer a good orchestra, from town.

She said abruptly, "Hadn't we better go back to our table?"

The place was filling up, becoming crowded. It was lucky that Tony had telephoned first.

After dinner they went out, the boy brought their car from the parking place and they started off over the twisting, tree-bordered roads which smelled of spring. And then somewhere between Ridgefield and Redding Tony turned off expertly and they traveled a rather bumpy and narrow road which turned and turned again and finally brought them to the open iron gates of Heron-crest, set high upon a ridge.

The house was stone, and enormous. The car lights shone briefly on gardens, coming into spring flower. "The pool's beyond," Tony explained, "behind that hedge." The trees stood back a little from the house, there was a flagstone terrace. Lights welcomed them, and as they went in and servants took their bags, Nelda came to meet them.

"We thought you were never coming," she said, in her slow, husky voice, and drew them into the warmth and flower-filled space of the big hall. "We're just having coffee," she went on, gesturing toward the living room. "Have you infants had dinner?"

"At Silvermine," said Tony.

"You could have come on out," she said, somewhat disapproving, smiled and took Linda in charge. "I'll take you to your room," she said. "Tony, your regular room's ready for you and you know the way."

Apparently, thought Linda, Tony had been

here often . . . since last autumn.

The gracious stairs curved upward, a landing with a huge picture frame plate-glass window interrupting them. Linda's room, when they reached it, was charming. A fireplace held logs to which a match had been touched recently. The color scheme was strange and striking: clear, pale turquoise and sudden unexpected notes of bright cherry. The bathroom had built-in dressing tables, an immense tub, a shower behind glass, and an array of bottles and jars which would have done Hollywood justice.

Nelda was tall and terribly thin in a long black dress. Her hair was remarkable, the pure, flawless gold seen so rarely out of childhood, and it fell about her pointed face, colorless but for the wide red mouth, as heavy and sleek and shining as satin. She said, "Don't bother to change, Linda, unless you'd rather. Come down and have coffee and — You don't know the Prestons, do you? We'll play contract or something," she said vaguely, "and I suppose people will drop in. They usually do. Tom's going to be late."

Left alone, Linda washed, did over her face, and put on the crepe frock. A glimpse through the living room archway had informed her that Mrs. Preston hadn't dressed. When she went down it was with the utmost reluctance. She didn't belong here, she thought. She wished she had not come. She could imagine Nelda explaining her to the Prestons . . . "works in Tony's office . . . such a nice little thing."

In Benfield, in her own place, she had been perfectly secure, and self-confident . . . until last winter. But this was alien territory. Here she had no background, no solid wall against which to lean. Here no one knew her, or cared. She thought fiercely, Well, you idiot, isn't that what you wanted, isn't that why you left Benfield?

The Peter Prestons were amiable and attractive people in their thirties. Peter was something or other in the Heron firm, his wife, Ann, was small, English, and very pretty. After the introductions and while Linda was drinking coffee and Tony prowling around the enormous room he asked, "What happened to Tom Yorke? I thought he'd be here."

"Blowout," said Nelda, "or at least that's what he said. He left town late, said he'd get something to eat on the way." She shrugged. "You know how he is."

They were listening to the radio and a servant was setting out a card table when Yorke arrived with a great screeching of brakes and came romping into the house. He was, Linda had long since decided, one of the oddest men she had ever met. A very brilliant young trial lawyer — an "A" man in his law classes — he appeared, on the surface, utterly irresponsible. But she knew his office record, which was difficult to reconcile with a number of things.

He embraced his hostess, patted Linda fondly on the head, and told Ann Preston that the only reason he had left town — as he loathed the country — was in order to see her again. He had a cup of coffee and two stiff drinks and suggested that the others play contract. "Linda and I," he remarked, "can sit this one out." There was a huge, screened sun porch beyond the living room, and he suggested that the radio might afford some dance music.

The evening passed in a kaleidoscopic manner. Neighbors came trooping in, several varieties of them: pretty young girls, two of them identical twins, a couple of stalwart boys who looked as if they should be in college but had probably graduated some years ago, a woman who looked more like a horse than a human being, a completely remote gentleman with a white beard who was probably her unfortunate husband. Another card table was set up, the identical twins took over the sun porch with their escorts. Drinks appeared and, later, sandwiches. Tom Yorke challenged Linda to table tennis in the game room downstairs and spent the entire time leaning on the table and inquiring plaintively why she never gave him a tumble. He said, "Just my luck to have you assigned to Powell. I'd spend more time in the office if they'd left you there."

When they went upstairs again they found the radio going full blast, two bridge tables occupied, and Nelda and Tony absent from the scene. Someone remarked that they had walked down to the pool and Yorke said unhappily, "Why didn't I think of that first?"

On Sunday morning Linda woke late and lay for a moment contemplating her surroundings. She felt sleepy and relaxed, and admired without much thought the sunlight on draperies and turquoise walls. When she had pulled herself together sufficiently she rose, performed sundry sketchy ablutions and then crawled back to bed, to ring for her breakfast as Nelda had bidden her do. "The women never get up," she had said, "too devastating. Besides, it gives the men a chance to talk about us . . . they can really let down their hair over coffee and ham and eggs or what have you."

Breakfast arrived, according to the order she had put in on the night before, coffee, fruit, toast. She ate it in a leisurely fashion, smoked a cigarette, turned on the bedside radio and listened to the nine o'clock news which was disheartening, a black shadow creeping over the bright sunlight of Sunday morning. Much later she put on her slacks, and as the day was warm, a round-collared linen shirt in which she looked no older than fourteen, and went downstairs. No one was in the living room or dining room but she found the Prestons and Tom Yorke on the terrace. Nelda and Tony, they reported, had gone riding. Nelda had left word that if Linda cared to ride — "with me," said Yorke, and added hopefully: "I hope you won't, as I despise any form of exercise" — there was a horse in the stables for her. "Masterpiece of understatement," added

Yorke, "as there are thousands of horses, all champing at the bit and yearning for a chance to give you the brush-off."

Linda said she didn't ride and Peter Preston suggested a tour of the grounds . . . or part of them, he amended, as they comprised some three hundred acres. "We'll stick to the trails of civilization," he promised.

Beautiful gardens, clipped hedges, and the pool behind its windbreak, with dressing rooms in a low white house, flagstones edging the very blue water. It was a big pool, cement, painted aquamarine, and jets of water rose and fell from the mouths of unlikely lions and dolphins. It was spring fed, Preston explained, and went on to talk of an intricate heating apparatus, underwater lights for night bathing, continuous flow of water for cleanliness, a scum gutter which really worked and so on. He ended thoughtfully that it probably cost the Herons a dollar a drop to maintain it.

Beyond were the utility units, garages, stables, barns, superintendent's cottage, servants' quarters. "Peace or war," said Preston, "Mr. Heron can maintain himself right here, provided he can get the requisite number of men to work for him. A thousand chickens, a herd of Jerseys, and plenty of space. They grow their own feed and vegetables. It's quite a setup. It costs plenty," he told Linda as they walked together; "it's Heron's baby. It could be run on a self-supporting basis, but isn't, of course."

Beyond she could see fields, stone walls and

woodlots, the trees showing the first tender, heartbreaking green. Flowering bushes were in bloom and the snowy rose, clear and delicate, of the fruit trees.

Presently Tony and Nelda came back from their ride and everyone went swimming. It had turned very warm toward noon, and the pool was a little warmer than the air. Linda protested that she had brought no suit but there was a stock of suits in the cabana, of all sizes, and a maid produced one which had not been worn.

Tom Yorke got himself into trunks, "because," he said proudly, "I have a very fine physique" — which was perfectly true — but refused to do more than dive once, swim to the end of the pool and climb out, wrapping himself in a sheet-sized towel and calling loudly for a drink. The sun shone on his sleek red head.

On the ledge at the far end of the pool Nelda and Tony were deep in conversation. Tony seemed to be protesting, perhaps too much, thought Linda, amused, as Nelda turned from him and in the middle of his sentence, plunged into the pool and swam away.

The course of true love, Linda thought.

Luncheon was served on the terrace, and afterward as Tony and Nelda had disappeared and Yorke seemed a little insistent, Linda excused herself and went to her room. She said, as Yorke chided her, "At my advanced age a twenty-minute nap is always indicated," and followed by his reproaches, went upstairs. She took off the slacks in which she had lunched and lay down on the bed. She thought, It's fun, it's an easy sort of life but it would bore me stiff in a little while. She would write her parents from here. She must write Alice Anderson. Alice wrote faithfully once a week. But her letters were so difficult to answer.

She began to think about the office, a change she had made in Powell's personal filing system. He had approved of it, as it was a short cut. She lay there, planning, thinking too that someday soon she must ask Cynthia to have dinner with her and go to a movie or something, and presently fell asleep. When she woke she knew by the altered light in the room that she had slept for some time. It must be nearly five. Well, no one had wakened her, so she had not been missed, she thought.

She got up feeling a little dazed from the heaviness of her sudden slumber, due, she supposed, to breathing pure air once more . . . and looked at her suitcase which was almost packed. They would not dress for dinner tonight, as they were all leaving shortly after dinner. So, presently, remembering that Nelda had said something about people dropping in for cocktails, she put on her suit and the thin sweater, and looked at herself in the glass. She was thinner, she thought, than when she had left Benfield. She liked the suit, muted pastel plaids, in a fine soft tweed, she liked her new haircut. She thought, But you could be one of a thousand girls, Linda.

Not like Nelda, for instance; there couldn't be any more like Nelda. I wonder, she asked herself, frowning at her reflection, why I don't like her. Not that I dislike her. It's as if there were nothing to like or dislike. And she's very nice to me . . . in a casual sort of way.

She went downstairs and guided by the sound of voices out to the sun porch. It seemed to be filled with people but for a split second there was only one person in it. No, two.

Rix Anderson stood there leaning against the mantel of the big stone fireplace with a glass in his hand and, just beyond him Peg, dark, sultry, in a startling red dress, was talking to Nelda.

Neither had seen her. Linda stopped where she was. She thought crazily, But this is like dying. She thought, I can't go in, I *won't*.

She made a supreme effort and turned away. She would go back, silently, creeping back upstairs, attaining the privacy and safety of her own room. There she would lock herself in until they had gone. Surely they would not be staying for dinner?

She had her back to them now. Someone touched her arm and turned her around. It was Tony. She felt the steadiness and warmth of his hand. She heard his voice, low, reassuring. She heard him say, for her alone, "No, that isn't the way, Linda." She felt the grasp tighten and heard his voice again, raised this time, for anyone to hear. "Where the devil have you been?" it de-

107

manded. "I thought you'd run out on us."

You can't run out, was what it really said, where's your pride? Don't be a fool, Linda, see this through.

She felt the blood come back into her veins. It was as if for a second she had been completely drained. She walked, still with Tony's hand on her arm, into the sun porch, saw Nelda step forward, saw Rix's utterly incredulous eyes, saw Peg's face turn very white.

"Linda," cried Nelda, "what on earth happened to you?" She turned to make the introductions but Linda spoke first, steadily. "We know each other. Hello, Peg," she said, "hello, Rix . . . how nice to see you."

That's right, be a hypocrite, watch the crazy relief in Peg's eyes, don't stop to wonder what Rix's expression means, take Peg's hand, and feel Rix touch yours again so briefly. He took her hand and dropped it almost at once. He said, "Of all the unexpected —"

Nelda made round eyes and Linda said, and somehow smiled, "But we're very old friends, Nelda. Rix is from Benfield too, you know."

Peg said, "I knew you were in town, Linda. Rix's mother wrote — I've been meaning to look you up, but things . . . You know how you never quite catch up in New York. We've just moved too, and that took a bit of doing."

Ann Preston spoke to her then, and Peg turned and Rix smiled. All the charm was there, all the vitality. A moment ago Linda had thought that he looked tired, even drawn. Before she could control it she had felt the instant concern, and anxiety. What was wrong, why did he look like that? It was habit, of course. You couldn't worry over a person for years and not go on worrying even when what they did or did not do was no longer any concern of yours.

"Linda," he said, "come here. There are a thousand things I want to ask you." He drew her away with him, touching her arm, and she looked for a moment at Tony, still standing beside her. His eyes met hers gravely. If they said anything at all, they said, This is up to you. You take over from here.

She found herself presently sitting beside Rix on a big swing in a corner of the sun porch. Someone brought her a cocktail and she took it mechanically and set it down beside her. And Rix said, astonished, "You never used to drink them."

Linda picked up the glass, drank a little and set it down again. She said lightly, "I've changed, I suppose," and took a cigarette from a silver box on a table beside her, lighted it and looked at him.

He said, "I — I don't quite know what to say, Linda."

"Suppose," she suggested evenly, "you don't say anything at all. Let's go on from here, shall we?"

He said, "Mother wrote me you were working in New York. She told me the firm name, and the address. I knew Tony Dennison was in the firm. We — met him, you know, at the Herons' one night last winter."

So it was at Nelda's that Tony had come in contact with Rix and Peg. Linda hadn't asked, she hadn't cared.

"My outfit," Rix explained, "handles some of Heron's private investments."

"I see."

"Linda," he said helplessly, "we can't go on from here. I mean we have to get things straight first."

She looked at him, full, and his eyes shifted and evaded her own. She said, "You haven't always reasoned that way."

"Don't you think I know? Don't you think I haven't known every day since and loathed myself," he said, "as you must despise me?"

She said coolly, "I haven't any feeling for you at all, Rix. Whatever I felt, it's over now. Quite. I made a good recovery," she added, with a sort of hard brightness, and wished with all her heart that it was not a lie.

"Linda," he begged, "if you knew how I felt — and Peg too. She was always fond of you. Isn't it possible," he asked, "for us to be friends?"

And restore your self-esteem, she thought, even set you right in your father's eyes . . . or a little right? Aloud, she said politely:

"I suppose it's possible, Rix, but I don't see much point in it."

Suddenly he was not looking at her. He was looking across the room and something came into his face that she had not seen for a long time, something young and amused and secret. She followed his regard. But he was not looking at Peg, now talking with a little too much animation to Tony Dennison. He was looking at Nelda, who was coming across to them. And Nelda was saying, "Can't you and Peg stay for dinner, Rix?"

He said, "I'd give anything to but you know we just sneaked away from the Jarrods' for an hour, they expect us back. We're not driving back until morning."

"I see," said Nelda, "I'm so sorry." She added, "Don't forget our date next week."

Presently Peg came over to them. She said, "Rix, you can't monopolize Linda like that when I have so much to ask her." But she hasn't, Linda thought. She doesn't want to see, much less talk to me, but she wants something or dislikes something else more than the situation. What is it? Then, watching Peg's regard slide across Nelda almost as if she weren't there, watching the sudden tightening of Rix's mouth, she knew. It was incredible. She thought, But they haven't been married six full months!

She didn't know whether she was glad or sorry. She told herself she didn't care, it was nothing to her. Yet looking up to see Tony frowning, as if in concentration, she wondered. And Nelda, smiling at Rix, Nelda's long eyes bright with amusement . . . What was she trying to do? thought Linda.

Suddenly she felt tired, flat. Well, it had happened. She had seen Rix again, and Peg. She had taken their hands, heard their voices, and all that she had dreaded had come to pass and she felt as if she had come a long way and was so tired she could not move another inch. Nothing mattered, she thought, I don't care any more. What had become of her love and her anger and her broken friendship? What had become of her grief and resentment and desperation? Here they were — Rix, with his brown eyes and his face more familiar to her than her own, Peg, with her dark, sullen loveliness — and yet the first shock having passed, they were as strange people whom she could watch with detachment.

Rix said, "Linda, you aren't very polite. I've spoken twice and you don't even hear me."

She said, with an effort, "I'm sorry, Rix, I was thinking of something else," and saw his instant blank amazement, its reflection on Peg's face, while Nelda looked curiously from one to the other.

"Rix," Nelda ordered, "come over here. There's something I want to show you."

Peg sat down beside Linda and watched her husband and Nelda walk away, both laughing, his head bent a little, to the smooth blond head, and said low, and unhappily:

"Why didn't you warn me, Linda . . . but then how could you?"

"Warn you — about what?" asked Linda slowly.

"That . . . he hasn't it in him to be loyal to anyone," said Peg, "not even to his wife."

Chapter 8

It was like being suspended in time; it was like finding yourself inside a magical crystal, you could look through, you could see the world outside, you heard voices, words, sentences, but you could not answer, you could not speak.

"I'm sorry," said Peg, "skip it. Forget I said anything."

The spell shattered, the crystal broke, and Linda came alive again. The room sprang into normal perspective, the voices in it seemed a little louder, that was all, and the colors sharper. She said quietly, "There are things you have to find out for yourself, Peg . . ."

"Hi," said Tony, appearing at Peg's elbow, "break it up, you two, and give a guy a chance. Linda, move over." As she obeyed, mechanically, he sat down between them and regarded Peg's empty glass. "How about more of the same?" he inquired, and took it from her.

"No, thanks," Peg told him, "we'll have to be getting back to the Jarrods'." She smiled at Tony, with, it appeared, no effort. "Mrs. J. is fearfully punctilious. Bells ring, for dressing, for meals. Very British. It's the biggest, stuffiest house you can imagine, and the Jarrods are period pieces. But we can't afford to offend them, as he's a very

114

lucrative customer."

In Benfield you didn't accept hospitality, then go to someone else's house and talk about your host and hostess. If you did and were overheard by a parent or an older friend, you were slapped down, hard. But this wasn't Benfield, Linda reflected. She wished with all her heart that it was. She wished herself back, in her own house, her own room, with her own people. If only you could wipe out six months, a year. But that wouldn't help. A year ago she and Rix —

Peg rose. She said, "Rix will have to tear himself away . . . business before pleasure." It was said lightly enough, but Linda's heart tightened. She watched Peg go across the room to stand with Nelda and Rix. Whatever she said, Rix protested. Linda could hear him, "Must we, angel," he demanded, "when this is so much more fun?"

She unclenched her hands. She had not been aware until this moment that they were little, tight fists, but now they ached and the fingers were cramped.

"Good girl," said Tony, low.

She turned, tried to smile into his concerned gray eyes. She said, "I'm sorry, Tony, I came within an inch of making a fool of myself. You see, I had no idea that Nelda knew Rix and Peg."

"I saw no reason to tell you," he said promptly, "and hadn't the foggiest notion that they'd be near here this weekend, much less barge in. If I had, I wouldn't have let you come, you know that. Yet, sooner or later, you were bound to run into them," he told her; "perhaps it's better to get it over, even without preparation."

"It's an absurd situation, isn't it?" she said. "Thanks for standing by."

"You look better," he said, "perhaps another drink . . . ?"

"No, I've had enough. I don't really like it," she said, "and I don't know why I bother. Perhaps because it's less trouble than refusing. What do you mean, I look better?"

He said, "I watched you from across the room. You were pretty white and strained."

Peg came back to them, with her slow, provocative walk. She asked, "Linda, may I speak to you a moment?"

Tony rose promptly. "Girlish prattle," he said, "that's what your father once called feminine chitchat in my hearing. I'll make myself scarce, although I burn with curiosity and am wounded to the quick. Sure I can't stay?" he asked Linda, laughing, but his eyes were grave and steady. Just say the word, they assured her, and Peg, together with whatever wild horses she may produce, couldn't drag me from this spot.

"Run along," ordered Linda, and drew a deep breath to quiet her heart.

When he had left, Peg said, "Linda, I simply have to see you. Can't we meet for lunch or something?"

Linda looked at her. "It doesn't make sense, Peg. We have nothing to say to each other."

Peg twisted one long, scarlet-tipped hand in the other. She said desperately, "I must . . . I have to talk to someone. Crazy as it sounds, you're the one human being I can talk to — I beg you to believe that. If I don't, I'll go crazy," she said in her exaggerated way. "I swear it."

What were Hecuba's tears to her? Linda thought. But curiosity came to life in her brain, a small, cold snake coiling and uncoiling. She thought, in horror, What sort of person have I become, that I want to hear what's wrong between them? Because something *is* wrong. Is it only because he's attentive to Nelda Heron?

After a moment she said, quietly:

"All right, Peg. Lunch is rather difficult. I don't go out at any specific time, it depends largely upon Mr. Powell. I'm supposed to get off at five, but don't, always, or I'd suggest tea somewhere. Would it be possible for you to come to the club?"

"You mean, does Rix ever leave me alone?" Peg's smile was sardonic. "Naturally," she said, "he's pretty occupied. You have to do battle for clients these days and you're apt to do it in bars, as well as on golf links. I'll call you at the office, if that's all right with you, and tell you when I'll be free."

"It's all right," began Linda, and then Rix stood beside them. She had not seen him come, but she felt it. He asked warily, "What are you two muttering about? I'm ready to go, Peg. You're behaving according to pattern," he informed her, "first all of a dither to get away and then, when I'm ready, holding up the procession."

Peg rose. She spoke to Linda without looking at him. "We'll get together sometime," she said easily. "It was fun seeing you. 'Bye, Linda."

Rix looked from one to the other. He stood easily, his hands in his pockets. "Sure, why not? Have dinner with us one night, Linda. We've a fair cook, and can show you a costly view of the East River. I selected the site because it will come in handy someday, when customers fade away and I feel impelled to jump in."

"A macabre but practical thought," said Linda evenly, astonished at herself, and rewarded by a flash of irritation and incredulity in Rix's dark eyes.

She watched them make their farewells to Nelda, the Prestons, to Tony and Tom Yorke. When they had gone she rose. She told Nelda, "I have some packing to do. We aren't dressing, are we?"

Nelda seemed abstracted. She said, "No, as we're leaving right after dinner. I'll come along up with you. You too, Ann? We can leave the men to their own mysterious devices."

They trailed upstairs, the small fair Englishwoman and Nelda, tall, too thin, the heavy gold of her hair about her shoulders. Ann was saying, "What an attractive couple. The Andersons, I mean."

"Yes," said Nelda, "amusing too. She's a bit

on the difficult side, rather moody, I think, but he's great fun. Isn't he, Linda?" She added to Ann, explaining, "Linda knows them very well."

"Rix and I were brought up together," said Linda, "and Peg and I were schoolmates." Well, she thought, there's a short, short story for you. P.S., home-town girl doesn't make good. She added, aloud, "Yes, they're fun."

Great fun, as Nelda had said. Screaming. They slew you. You were prone in the aisle for anyone to step on.

Linda finished her packing — there was little of it — lit a cigarette and sat down in a big chair to think this through. To what had she committed herself? She'd been a fool. She need never see Rix or Peg again, certainly not of her own volition. But Peg was unhappy. Good, said Linda savagely to herself. Peg had, in New England parlance, received her comeuppance. And why shouldn't she?

Habit's a crazy thing. They had been very close friends; and now, in her unhappiness, Peg had turned to Linda. A wonderful friend she turned out to be! thought Linda. So what? So I'm supposed to say, There, there, it's all right, what can I do to make you feel better . . . kiss the bruise and make it well? Well, I can't, she told herself, I haven't grown a halo. I don't hate her. I just don't like her any more. I don't want to have anything to do with her — or with him.

Rix, it was dreadful seeing you again. It was

unreal, it was fantastic, you were as remote from me as the stars. Yet I kept remembering. You can't love a man for years and years and not remember. Habit's not only crazy, it's cruel and malicious. Your mind tells you, This man is nothing to you, the man you loved never really existed or this wouldn't have happened; he never really loved you or he wouldn't today be married to the girl who was once your best friend. Yet the pulses didn't know that. They hadn't been informed with the power to think. The blood in your body didn't reason, it was shaken and disturbed, no matter what the brain said, coolly, logically.

"It's such a mess," said Linda aloud, and put her head in her hands and cried and cried from sheer nerves and reaction.

She had washed her face and done it over when the knock came at her door. She went to open it and Tony was there. He asked, "How about a hand of gin rummy, before dinner?" Then he broke off and looked at her closely. "You've been bawling," he accused her sternly.

Linda smiled, after a diluted fashion. She didn't mind Tony's knowing somehow. She said, "Silly of me, wasn't it? I suppose it was just nerves and all that."

He said, "Well, damn it, he isn't — I mean, they aren't worth it."

"What does that matter?" she asked soberly and went out of the room and downstairs to be soundly trounced for three games before dinner was announced.

They left shortly after dinner was over, following arguments as to the distribution of man power in the three cars. Nelda settled it. She and Tony in his car, the Prestons in hers, and Tom could take Linda. Linda's heart lightened a little because Tony was obviously so pleased. She didn't mind being shuffled around. Tony was such a good guy, she told herself, he deserved a break. Nelda hadn't given him much time over the weekend. She thought, Maybe she's really fond of him. He's insane about her, and it would be a good marriage. There can't be anything in this absurd business with Rix.

Tony's worth ten of Rix, she informed herself, and besides, Rix is *married.*

Benfield spoke there, common decency and all her background of tradition and fair play . . . the tradition Peg had violated.

It was, she found, difficult to adjust herself to present circumstances. She wrote Alice Anderson, because she felt she must. A harder letter had never been composed. In the end it was simple enough, a statement of fact. She had gone to a weekend house party in Connecticut and had seen Rix and Peg. They looked very well.

Alice's reply, in her large, angular script, came by return mail. She wrote, "I'm grateful to you for telling me. But, poor child, it must have been very hard for you."

More pity. Linda crumpled the letter in her

hand. Oh, let them forget, she prayed, let me get over it.

Get over what? Not Rix's betrayal nor Peg's treachery alone, but the softness in herself, the weakness, she told herself fiercely, which made her keep on wanting to trust people, to care for them, to have friends. Tony didn't count. He was good, he was honest, she could swear to that, and he was in love with someone else. In any event she was immune so far as men were concerned. Tom Yorke while driving her home from Heroncrest had debated that with her. He said when, due to his urgency, they had stopped at a roadside place for coffee and a sandwich — "After all that dinner?" she'd demanded, and he had responded, "It's only an excuse" — and danced a little to the juke box, "You don't look like a cold critter, darling."

"I," said Linda firmly, "am the Ice Queen herself."

"If I recall my fairy tales, even she melted."

They were dancing. Linda kept step smoothly. She asked, " 'Who's afraid of the big bad wolf?' "

"So that's what you think? If you gave me the slightest encouragement, Linda, my intentions might even be honorable." He went on, in some astonishment, "Although it's a regrettable thought, as I don't want to marry — the mere idea frightens me. One household, one woman, pipe, slippers, and a sleepy dog. A couple of kids, not sleepy enough. Golf on

Sundays and dinner at the in-laws —"

"We could hardly run up to Benfield for Sunday dinner," she reminded him demurely.

"Well, that's something. My people, then. All very correct and stuffy. My mother's cute," he said, "and southern. But her aunt lives with us and she's pre-Civil War. You know, faithful black mammies, ye old plantation, dripping mint juleps, Spanish moss, and a little black boy to fan you. Seventeen-inch waists, the family silver buried in the back yard and *that* Sherman. It's pretty dreadful. You must come up and see us sometime. I'll say you're from New England by way of, let's see . . . Virginia, would do."

She'd laughed. She had asked, "How about Nelda?"

"Oh, Nelda," said Tom carelessly, "every man who meets her goes through a phase. He falls in love, he despairs, he is harrowed. Then one morning he wakes up free as air. She's got what it takes at first sight, so to speak, but you soon find you're astigmatic. You see, Nelda's peculiar charm lies in the fact that she appears so mysterious, so Melisande in the wood. She has that quality, rather rare, very intriguing. Still water, all that sort of thing. Then when you come to know her you realize there isn't anything there at all. No depths which you alone might plumb. Nothing but a parrot brain which repeats the catch phrases of the era correctly, in the right places, to the right people and — an overwhelming vanity."

"Golly," said Linda, "how hard she must have turned you down!"

"Why, you little brat," he said, exasperated, "that's no way to win a man — by telling him the truth."

"I don't want to win you," she said, "not even in a raffle."

"Smart girl." Yorke sighed. "No, Linda, Nelda was a temporary aberration. She's in love with two things, irrevocably. Herself, for one; and her attraction for men. Poor old Tony."

"Tony?" She wouldn't discuss Tony with Tom. Tony was her friend. The only friend on whom she could rely.

"Sure. He has a very bad case. Prognosis doubtful," said Yorke. "The odd thing is I think she likes him as well as she's capable of liking anyone . . . she might even marry him at that. Wretched thought. After about three months he'd wake out of his dream and howl dismally, like a dog. Of course she has her — moments. That cinemapuss Anderson, for instance. Methought I saw the old familiar gleam in her eye. Only more so. What do you think?" he inquired. "You used to hang over the garden gate with Anderson, or so I heard."

Linda said evenly, "Yes, I've known him always. And Peg's an old friend." There was no hesitation between adjective and noun. She went on, "But I'm sure you're mistaken. Rix is very attractive —" too attractive, said her heart — "but he's been married a very short time. Not that the length of time makes any difference to this discussion. Let's just say, he's married."

Yorke grinned. "For a kid who's been in town for half a year, you are certainly incredibly naïve. Nelda doesn't care if a man's married. She doesn't care about anything but her effect upon him. If ever she runs into one and starts to consider his effect upon her, well, it's just going to be too bad, for her, for good old Tony, and for the gentleman's wife, provided he has one."

Which, reflected Linda afterward, certainly gave one furiously to think.

Life went on, the early summer was unseasonably warm, and Peg had not called her on the telephone. Perhaps she never would, thought Linda, relieved. She and Cynthia went about together, she enjoyed being with Cynthia, but refused to permit the friendship to be more than casual, with no demands on either side. There wasn't a woman in the world she'd trust. Never again. You didn't let yourself in for that twice, she thought. Not that history could repeat itself. It was simply that she didn't want to know Cynthia too well, nor to confide in her, nor to receive confidences in return.

Her work at the office was good, Mr. Powell was pleased. She made no friends. Possibly the other secretaries and clerks were a trifle disappointed in her. She was pleasant, but she gave none an opportunity for intimacy. She did not often lunch with them, in groups, nor did she linger in the rest room for gossip, conjecture, banter. This naturally did not endear her to the girls her own age. It did, however, endear her to Miss Covert, whose position as personnel head of the female employees had endowed her with the discipline of a drill sergeant and a consciousness of royalty that is otherwise given only to an American woman who marries a title. What Miss Covert did not know was that Linda had no intention of being a secretary all her life. She fully intended to take a night law course in the autumn and thus more than equip herself for Miss Covert's position when that lady was ready — if ever — to retire.

She had dined occasionally with Miss Covert in the older woman's pleasant apartment, she lunched with her now and then, and told herself sternly that qualms were absurd and reactionary, out of place, and set herself, single-mindedly, to extracting from Miss Covert all the information possible about the job. The more she knew the better off she'd be when the time came.

She was beginning to believe that she would not hear again from Peg Anderson when Peg telephoned one morning to the office. She said breathlessly, "I haven't had a chance before. May I come to your club late this afternoon, or could we have dinner together somewhere? Rix is out of town."

Linda had a good and reasonable excuse. As a matter of fact, she was having dinner with Tom

Yorke and going on to a movie. He had been very attentive . . . although he had not again referred to their conversation of the evening driving back to New York, except in oblique ways.

She said, "I have a dinner engagement; I'll have to get myself home and dress."

"Let me come while you dress," said Peg. "Please, Linda. It's so important — at least to me."

It wasn't the first time Linda had dressed and Peg had sat in her room with her or lain full length on the bed or walked about smoking, talking, laughing. Linda thought, Get it over with. Besides, she wanted to know; she fiercely desired to hear with her own ears what Peg had to say and to watch her face as she said it. She said, "All right, Peg, I think I can be back at the club by five-thirty." She gave the address, hung up and went back to her work.

She thought, What can she possibly tell me? That Rix is interested in Nelda? What difference can that make to me? She's made her bed, thought Linda, her little jaw set, she can lie in it — with misery for her pillow.

Tony poked his head in at the door. He asked, "Alone? Where's his Highness?"

"You know perfectly well that he's in court."

"So he is. *Smith v. Renwick Company.* Boy, what a dull morning he'd have." Tony advanced into the anteroom and shut the door firmly behind him. "Congratulate me," he said, "I'm an engaged man."

"Tony, you're not!"

"I certainly am." He sat down on the edge of her desk and swung his long legs. His mouse-colored hair was wildly disheveled, he had cut himself shaving, and his gray eyes were bright with excitement. "It's going to be announced next week. Big shindig at the future in-laws. You're asked."

"I'm so glad for you," she said. She was. He was happy. It was wonderful to see anyone so happy. He looked, she thought, as she had once felt. She said, "It's Nelda, of course?"

"Who else could it be?" he demanded, astonished. "I'm the luckiest guy in the world. I was beginning to chafe at the bit, wondering if a mere lawyer could join the RAF. My God, Linda, so much afoot in the world and me not in there pitching. My draft number's so high it needs an oxygen mask. No kiddin' . . . but this changes things a bit. And she's pretty wonderful."

"Of course," said Linda, and thought, I wish it was anyone else but Nelda . . . he's too good for her. I feel it, in my bones.

He got up, came over and dropped a kiss on the top of her head. "Youngster," he said, "I wish things were as good for you as they are for me." He looked at her, with real anxiety. "Tom's been telling me he thinks you're pretty special."

"Oh, Tom!"

"You could do worse. He'll settle down and shed the wolf disguise. He's a very brilliant young man," said Tony, "and I'm the one to know it."

"He's all right," said Linda.

He said, "One nail drives out another. He'd be fun even if you don't take him seriously. You know, I wish I could see you again as I did the first time I ever set eyes on you . . . bubbling over with a sort of inner joy, so enchanting to see. Made me envious of the —" He broke off. "I didn't mean to say that, I'm a clumsy fool. And I've hurt you."

"No, you haven't," she said, "you couldn't." She swung around and gave him her hand. "When are you going to be married?" she asked.

He shrugged, frowned. "Nelda's a brat," he told her. "Not until around Christmas, a million years away."

"Why?"

"I don't know. She says it's too soon. She's very young, you know," he added tenderly.

"Is your mother pleased?" asked Linda.

"She's delighted. Anything that makes me happy goes with her, of course. And she and Nelda get along beautifully. Which reminds me for no good reason that I have to see a client, now, this minute."

The telephone rang on Linda's desk and a voice inquired severely, "Is Mr. Dennison in Mr. Powell's office, Miss Wheaton? Mr. Mather is waiting to see him."

"Your cue," said Linda, "a Mr. Mather."

Tony nodded. He said, "And then, before I lunch with one of God's gifts to lawyers — Litigation Louis, we always call him . . . he's in and out of courts as a cuckoo a clock — before Louis, I have to nip out to the florist. I suppose girls get tired of orchids."

"It's June," said Linda smiling, "why not send her something Junelike along with the orchids?"

The door closed behind him. Linda sat quite still at her desk. She would miss Tony. She'd see him every day but it would be different. Why? She had never known him when he was fancy free save for that brief time in Benfield. But a fiancée was bound to make a difference.

She sighed, and picked up a letter she had just written. It seemed to make sense. She thought, I wish today would last forever so I need not see Peg, not ever; she thought, I wish it was five and I was on my way home.

Chapter 9

She waited in the lounge for Peg. Girls wandered in and out, the radio was playing. The lounge was bright with late sunlight, shining on pleasant chintz; the windows stood open to the wind. Linda looked at her watch. She's late, of course, she's always late, she thought.

She stopped to talk to a group of girls, killing time over a game of contract. Linda knew a number of the club residents by now. This one, a pretty blonde, was a young actress; she hadn't had a part for six months; she had landed one only that morning; color was high in her cheeks, a flag of triumph; the dark, sullen girl sang; she had considerable means, studied with one of the best teachers in town; her parents were nervous, refused to permit her to have her own apartment. Her partner was the girl from Ohio who roomed next door to Linda. She had lost her job a week ago, was looking for another. She cried at night, and Linda heard her. The fourth was a newcomer: she was fresh out of college and her job with a fashion magazine was to begin the first of the coming week.

Linda moved toward the door. She thought, Perhaps she won't come. Then suddenly there she was, the superb figure, the sultry loveliness,

131

the low-pitched voice asking for Miss Wheaton.

Linda went forward. She said, "Suppose we go up to my room — I don't have to dress for a time. My engagement's at eight."

Peg looked casually about the lounge as they passed it. She said, "This is quite a place."

"Sun deck, everything," said Linda, trying to smile and to talk naturally. "It's very pleasant, really."

"Too many women, I'd go crazy shut up with a lot of females," commented Peg.

They went upstairs in silence. When the door had shut behind them Peg cast her hat upon the bed, ran her hand over her sleek, shining hair.

"Smoke," she asked, "or is it against rules?"

"Sit down," said Linda, "that's the best chair. Ash tray on the windowsill." She sat down on the bed, the pillows against her back. She asked, after a moment, "Well, Peg?"

"Now that I'm here I don't know how to begin," said Peg, and flushed darkly.

"Perhaps," said Linda evenly, "it was a mistake to come. We can — let it go at that, if you like."

"I don't like. Linda, there's no one to whom I can talk, no one. You must listen. You're the best friend I ever had . . ." She broke off. She wasn't especially sensitive, but the sound of her own words appalled her.

"I was," said Linda, with a slight emphasis.

"All right," said Peg, and it was as if illogical anger stirred and drove her on, "let's get it over. All those last months, Rix and I behind your back

132

. . . It was easy. You were utterly unsuspicious. You were as happy and guileless as a child. Don't think it didn't make me sick. It did. I liked you, more than I'd ever liked any girl. But it didn't matter, very much. I was crazy, I was in love, nothing mattered but Rix. At first, a sort of flirtation. We were wary, we kept telling each other, all in good clean fun. Then it wasn't fun any more, it wasn't good nor," she said, low, "clean. The first time he came to see me at Mrs. Smith's — She was away for the weekend. She gave me the run of the house anyway. There wasn't a soul at home. The maid was off too. I said I'd eat out, do my own room, give her a chance to have a little holiday. That night Rix and I were at your house for dinner, we went to a movie later. It was the time Tony Dennison was in Benfield. You all took me home. Rix went home with you and then he came back to Smith's."

"Oh no," said Linda, on a half whisper.

"Yes. Remember near Christmas, trimming the tree, I went to pieces? I acted like a fool. I couldn't help it. I was desperate. You were to be married soon, Rix had never said anything to indicate that he wouldn't go through with it. From the very first he hadn't known he'd get in so deep. When he realized it, he told me over and over that nothing could be done about it. He loved me, but he was very fond of you; your parents and his expected this marriage, their hearts were set on it, his hands were tied. Right up to the last he kept saying that —"

Linda said, low, "It would have been kinder, Peg, if, when it first began, Rix had come to me and asked me to release him, told me he didn't want to marry me."

"He doesn't face things," said Peg. After a moment she said, "Well, I made him, I told him I was pregnant."

Linda was very white.

"I wasn't," said Peg defiantly. "But I made him see what it would mean — scandal, everything. I said I would go to his father."

"Did you ever believe that you were?" asked Linda. Her voice was as hard, as cold and smooth as a stone wrested from frostbound earth.

"No," said Peg sullenly. "But I knew what he wanted. He wanted me. He didn't want you and Benfield, Linda. But he was afraid to say so."

"And — did you tell him that you had lied?" asked Linda inexorably.

Peg's gray eyes shifted, looked away. She said, "Yes, of course, afterward. It didn't matter then, we were married, we were together, we were happy."

She's lying now, thought Linda contemptuously. She's never told him. Oh, some excuse . . . anything. Merely that she was mistaken, after all. But she hasn't told him that it was a deliberate lie on her part. Her heart was tight with a species of triumph. She had Peg now, she could tell Rix if she wished, tell him right out, she lied to you, she blackmailed you into marriage.

What good would that do? she thought.

Peg said, "We were happy, at first. He liked New York, he still does; and his work; and the people he meets. If there weren't another woman in the world we'd still be happy. But there are other women. There's Nelda Heron, for instance."

"What about her?"

"She's insane about him," said Peg, "or as much as she can be. And he is about her. That's all there is to it. I know it. He hates me for it. We quarrel a good deal of the time." She turned away, stared out the window. "If I had any guts I'd leave him. Tomorrow. I'd go to Reno, I'd divorce him." She swung back. "I can't," she cried. "I'm in love with him, it would kill me."

Linda felt chilled, as if her veins ran thin red ice. She said, "I think you're mistaken about Nelda's being interested in Rix. She's engaged to Tony Dennison. It's to be announced shortly, they'll be married next winter sometime."

"Tony Dennison?" said Peg. She laughed, a short harsh sound. "What difference does that make?"

"But if she's in love with Rix," began Linda, "why would she —"

"You're still pretty young," said Peg coolly. She surveyed Linda. "You — dress differently, you make up a little more, you're thinner. You know all the answers, apparently. I heard you talking at Nelda's. But underneath you're the same. Nelda doesn't want to *marry* Rix. He's nobody. A young man in a brokerage office. He'll always be that," said Peg bitterly, "even when he's old. A young-old man in someone's office. But Tony Dennison's a clever lawyer. He's been made a junior partner in a big and famous firm. He'll go places. That's what Nelda wants. She doesn't have to marry for money, she has all the money in the world, more or less. But she wants to marry someone — and not too long out of her first season — who is ambitious, whom she can push. Politically, perhaps. I've heard her talk. With her father's backing and the sort of hostess she'd be, she could do a lot for Tony if he wants to play it that way. If I divorced Rix tomorrow she wouldn't have him. Besides, you know the Herons — or don't you? They have odd prejudices for people of their type. One thing they don't happen to like is divorce. If Nelda married a divorced man, they'd cut her off with a shilling or whatever it is. No. She'll marry Tony and she'll push him for all she is worth, and that's plenty, and if another man happens to take her fancy, whether it's Rix or anyone else, she'll amuse herself on the side, very discreetly."

"I don't believe it," said Linda slowly.

"Don't take my word for it," said Peg. "She's been clever about Rix. I'm usually around. Oh, he's seen her for lunch and, I think, on other occasions. But he always tells me afterward, they just ran into each other, that sort of thing. After she's married it will be the same."

Linda said, "Tony doesn't deserve that. He's one of the best."

Peg leaned forward. She said, "Why don't you
—" She broke off. Then she asked curiously,
"You're interested in Tony yourself, aren't you?"

"No," said Linda, "I'm not." Her blue eyes
met Peg's squarely. "I like him. He's fine, he's a
good friend."

"Then," said Peg, "you're still in love with Rix?
Why not admit it? It doesn't matter now . . . and
it wouldn't do you any good," she said brutally,
"against Nelda Heron. He'll always have a — a
feeling of humiliation toward you. He hates you
for it, because it was his fault. That's the way he
is. He's the sort of man who can borrow from
someone and despise the man the rest of his life
because he's under an obligation, a burden of
gratitude. No; you're washed up," she said. "I
succeeded in that, pretty well. Now it's Nelda
and my turn."

"You don't expect me to be sorry," said Linda,
"do you? For you, I mean."

"No," said Peg, "I don't. You hate me, don't
you, Linda?"

"No," said Linda truthfully. "I did, once. At
first. Not now. I'm indifferent to you, Peg."

"But not to Rix?"

Linda was silent. She thought, Deny it, look
her in the eye, say, Rix is nothing to me now,
and never will be again.

"Okay, okay," said Peg impatiently, "you don't
have to answer. You have a hangover, I suppose.
Rix is like that. You get drunk on him and then
comes the awakening and you're still drunk in a

horrible, sickening sort of way."

Linda said, "I don't see why you came to me . . ."

"You can tell Tony . . ." began Peg. Then she shook her head. "What good would that do? He wouldn't believe you, he'd think you were being catty or jealous . . . he knew all about you and Rix. No, there's nothing you can do, and I didn't come to ask you to do anything. I came because I had to tell someone. I'm half out of my mind, with jealousy. Maybe it won't last. Maybe he'll be himself tomorrow. Maybe he'll get over it and forget. He's like that, I think. But suppose he doesn't. Suppose he keeps on with it, even after she's married? Because she'll make it plausible. She'll tell him, if not in so many words, You aren't free, we can't be married, even if you could free yourself, it wouldn't be any good because of my family. So I'm marrying Tony Dennison."

"On what excuse?" asked Linda scornfully.

"A dozen. Her family wants her to, it's time she married. Maybe if she marries Tony she'll forget Rix. All that sort of thing. Simple enough. And it will go on under Tony's nose and mine. Only he's so besotted he won't see it and she'll take good care to keep him that way. I'll see it," said Peg, "and I can't do anything about it. Rix hates scenes. I've made them. Someday if I make one too many he'll walk out on me." Suddenly she dropped her head in her hands and a dry sobbing shook her, dreadful to hear. She said, gasping, "I can't help it, Linda. I love him very much. I'd — I'd let him trample on me if it would do any good. I know what he's like. There's nothing in him to admire or respect, he's weak and he's treacherous, he's a complete egotist . . . selfish . . . unkind. But I keep on loving him. That's my punishment, I suppose."

"Yes," said Linda slowly, "I suppose it is."

She looked at Peg. It was growing darker now, the long and golden dusk of summer. She said, after a moment, "I suppose I ought to thank you."

Peg lifted her face and stared at the other girl. Her eyes were dry and her cheeks. But her face looked as ravaged as though she had wept for days on end, as perhaps she had.

"Thank me?" she repeated blankly.

"Yes. Seeing you and Rix was a shock," said Linda carefully. "I didn't think I could go through with it . . . I had hated you both. If you think you have lost him now, Peg, well, I lost him, and there was no if or but about it, was there? I had known him a great many years, you had known him a short time. I had put down very deep roots. I had to tear them up. It hurts. Seeing him again, so much I thought I had forgotten came back. You can't help remembering, after all those years, and I had been so happy . . ."

She was silent, contemplating that odd state of vanishing Nirvana, complete happiness, selfless, serene . . . she looked back on the girl who had wanted nothing but Rix, a home, Rix's children and their life in Benfield together. Nothing but that . . . and yet it had seemed all the world.

"You see," she said, over Peg's murmur, "in my heart I felt it was my fault. That I hadn't been desirable — enough; because I couldn't keep him . . . something must have been lacking in me. Eventually I told myself that, over and over. It made me uncertain, insecure. It was a final sort of abasement. But if you can't either," she said, her eyes widening, "it doesn't lie in us, but in him. And you've made me see him, perhaps as he is, and now I'm free —" she rose from the bed and went to stand by the window looking out without seeing — "free as air; as if I had dropped a burden I hated carrying and had to conceal from other people."

Peg said after a minute, "That's all very well, but what happens to me?"

Linda said, "I don't know. Frankly, I don't care."

"But that isn't like you," Peg began. She too remembered. Linda, her heart so vulnerable to pain, so sensitive to another's need. Linda, who always wanted the runt of a litter of pups because no one else would want it, who would nurse a sick animal back to life, who was tender with children and old people and growing things. Who could perform unpleasant tasks for people, hating the tasks but loving the people more.

"It's like me now," said Linda.

Peg rose. She said wearily, "I don't know why I came. I thought you'd say something that would help. You've said, yourself, how long you'd known him. I thought maybe you knew the formula . . ."

"If I had known it," said Linda evenly, "would you have managed to marry him, Peg?"

"I never thought of that," said Peg dully. She turned to go. She said, "You're bound to run into us, Linda. Especially now that Tony and Nelda are engaged. It can't be helped. She asks us everywhere. We go because it's supposed to be good business. The connection with her father. I tell you, my hands are tied. I'm —"

"Warning me?" asked Linda, and found herself laughing. "You needn't. You helped me, very much. I don't care how often I encounter you, Peg, or Rix. Because it's over. I know that definitely, for the first time since it all happened."

She went to the door, and added, "I'll go downstairs with you."

Peg said, "Wait. I told Rix I was coming here. I said I wanted to make it up with you."

"I'm sure," said Linda, "that he was delighted."

"Oh, don't bother being sarcastic," said Peg. "He was, as a matter of fact. Not that he'll ever see you without feeling uneasy. He's beginning to feel that way about me now too. I know the symptoms. If he was strong, in even the wrong way, then he wouldn't care. He wouldn't care how often he met you, he wouldn't care what I guessed or felt. But he isn't strong in any way.

And he does care because it destroys his own image of himself."

"What are you going to tell him?" asked Linda.

"That's up to you."

"Tell him," said Linda, "that it's all right. That I don't hold it against him or you, so far as I'm concerned we're just buddies."

"I loathe this," said Peg sharply.

"What? I thought you'd like it."

"Hearing you say things like that. I was crazy to come here. But even after what I did, I've always felt I could go to you. You were always so honest, clear through. That was what tortured me all that time before —"

"It didn't torture you sufficiently," Linda said.

"No," said Peg. "You meant a lot, but Rix meant very much more. He still does. More than anything, more than my pride, more than my regret. That's my own private hell."

Linda's heart twisted. She knew that signal. She tried to ignore it and could not. No one can change as completely as she had thought, not basically. As if without her own volition, her hand was on Peg's arm. She said, "I — I am sorry."

"Yes," said Peg slowly, "I guess you are. You're still — around, aren't you? No, don't go with me, I'll find my way alone."

She had gone and Linda stood at the open door. Then she went into the room, closed the door and lay full length on her bed. She thought, in simple childlike terms, It serves her right. She thought, Perhaps it's worse for her, she's married to him, she's his *wife*. I wasn't . . . I was just in love with him, always.

But not now.

It was wonderful, not being in love, to be able to think back, to remember and not have it matter. Peg had come to her for an impossible word of advice or consolation. She had come almost reluctantly but wistfully, as a child — the girl who had seemed as if she had never been a child but born armored in adult beauty, in easy sophistication. Now she'd gone, empty handed. But she had brought gifts with her, without knowing.

Linda was free, she was her own again. She could work and play and have fun and there would be no shadow. She was secure again. Because it hadn't been her fault. The fault must lie in Rix himself, if Peg could not hold him, Peg whom he had loved enough to marry.

Or had he? Had it been because of Peg's little scheme, so simple, so sordid, so terrifying to a man like Rix — or would that compel almost any man?

Well, that didn't matter either. She, thought Linda, has ten times my looks and fifty times my sex appeal. She's smooth and lovely and smoldering. She's exciting. I wasn't, not ever. But now he doesn't want her any more. He wants Nelda.

She had forgotten about Nelda and Tony for the moment. She thought, Nelda can't, she mustn't . . .

Not Tony. He was too decent, too much in love. He wouldn't get over a hurt easily. He would never get over it, not that kind of hurt. She thought, I can't do anything.

Yet could she not? Perhaps there were things she could do. Divert Rix's attention? Impossible. Yet would it be, perhaps, once he was assured that she cared nothing for him, was all over that nonsense?

She switched on the lights, looked in the mirror, at the bright, tumbled hair, the blue eyes, the curving mouth. She thought, I'll see them — as much as I can, all of them. Rix and Peg, Nelda and Tony. And if I think Peg's right, if Nelda means to go on with it, if she means to hurt Tony, I'll do something about it.

What?

She didn't know.

Back in Benfield when Tim Wheaton's daughter said she'd do something about it, she did. She managed somehow. She would again.

You had one friend. One person you could trust. For that person you could accomplish the impossible.

Someone knocked at her door. Linda had a telephone call. When she reached the instrument she heard Nelda's voice, like Château Yquem . . . it had the pale-gold quality, the iced sweetness.

"Linda? Tony's told you, of course. . . . Yes, isn't it? . . . Wednesday night . . . not many people. I'm writing the invitations now, but I wanted to be sure that you — You will come, won't you?"

"Of course," said Linda, "I wouldn't miss it for worlds. I hope you and Tony will be very happy, Nelda."

Hanging up she thought grimly, He'd better be or I'll know the reason why.

Perhaps Peg was mistaken. She was corroded with jealousy. It might be entirely in her mind, Nelda's share in this unpleasant business. Simply because Rix was attracted Peg would think that Nelda must be too. She was as much in love with him as that. I'll find out, said Linda to herself, I'll find out.

She had spoken aloud. Cynthia, into whom she ran full tilt, asked, "Hey, what's cookin'? Are you talking to yourself?"

"I love a good audience," Linda said, smiling. "I must fly. I have to dress for a date. I could do with a mild orgy tonight."

"What's happened to you?" asked Cynthia.

Linda grinned. "Plenty," she said, and thought, But it isn't a patch on what's going to happen to other people if Peg's telling the truth.

Chapter 10

Nelda's announcement party was on the memorable side. Her parents gave the engagement dinner for her on the St. Regis Roof, a setting which was most becoming to Nelda, sheathed in fluid gold, from golden head to golden slippers. Tony's ring was a ruby and she wore other rubies, the color of her mouth, at her throat and around her wrists, in the antique gold settings in which they had been presented to her by her maternal grandmother.

Tom Yorke called for Linda and whistled appreciatively when he met her in the club lounge. She had gone into her trousseau for a frock she had not yet worn. She had not been able to endure wearing it, for Rix had selected the color from samples Peg had brought from New York to Benfield, a thousand years ago. It was the blue of her eyes, simply made, on lovely lines, and girdled in silver. Tom commented, putting her in the car, "One of the prettiest girls who ever gladdened these old eyes, dear."

She asked, "Woollcott speaking? Thanks very much. Golly, it's hot tonight . . . I understand Nelda is leaving for Southampton when this announcement business is over."

"Is she? My people will be there," said Tom,

"in the stuffiest house you've ever seen, unless it's the town mausoleum. I suppose I'll go down weekends, whenever I can, and of course Tony will be at the Herons'."

"Why do the Herons want the Connecticut house?"

"Oh, for one of those weekend pied-à-terres," said Tom, laughing: "autumn, spring, or a run up now and then for skiing, when they aren't in Palm Beach. The Southampton place isn't large but it's a honey. The old man likes his fishing, golf, and surf bathing. The Connecticut jernt is really Mrs. Heron's baby."

"Why," asked Linda, "do people find it necessary to live in so many houses?"

"Well, for one thing," said Tom, "it affords them a topic of conversation: 'You know, my dear, I have to open the Florida place and close the Long Island shack and of course run up to Connecticut to talk about the storm windows.' . . . It's going to be a little more difficult," he added, "to maintain all these dilatory domiciles, what with domestic servants deciding defense work's the thing, the draft and all the rest of it, not to mention taxes. By the way, did I tell you you are looking very pretty tonight?"

"Yes," said Linda, "you did, and thank you again."

He said, "You couldn't by any chance be falling in love with me, could you?"

"Perish the thought," Linda answered cheerfully.

"That's funny," he said. "I thought I was just your type."

They reached their destination, and Linda waited in the lobby while Tom wrestled with the problem of parking. He ended by putting the car in a West Side garage and taxiing furiously to the St. Regis. When he returned Linda was talking to Peg and Rix Anderson. Only Peg, with her blue-black hair, dark skin and gray eyes, could have managed to wear a dress of sheer orange chiffon, startling in line and color.

They'd arrived almost as soon as Linda and Rix had hailed her. He'd said, as if delighted, "Linda, this *is* luck." He'd added, "Don't I recognize that dress? It's very attractive."

He spoke, doubtless, without thinking why and how he recognized it, for almost as soon as he had asked the question, he looked disturbed, and Peg said, with the ease of a knife sliding into butter, "You should, darling, you selected the color, and I had the dress made for her."

She looked from one to the other and Linda said lightly, and quite without effort, "That's the one, Rix — from the well-remembered trousseau. Don't look so upset. I don't feel the least compunction — or nostalgia — wearing it."

"Lord," he said, with a rueful smile, "I certainly put my foot in it this time, didn't I?"

"Why?" asked Linda. "Aren't you being a little self-conscious about the whole thing?"

She was certainly not self-conscious. Rix Anderson felt a curious admixture of relief and chagrin. He said, "She's a good sport, isn't she, Peg?"

"Wonderful," said Peg. "And that remark was certainly not Emily Post either."

"Oh, you two," said Linda, and her tone was much as it once had been, half affectionate, half tolerant, "you're being very silly. Why don't you go up to the party? Tom's probably having difficulty parking, he'll be along any time now. I'll wait here."

"You and Yorke . . ." began Rix, rallying.

She interrupted, smiling, "No speculations. There's a columnist under my chair. After all, Tom's rather well known."

He looked at her with bewildered admiration.

"You've come a long way," he commented.

"Isn't that Dietrich?" Linda asked Peg. "Look — going into the elevator. Of course it is. I didn't know she was in town."

They were still discussing celebrities and the cinema when Tom, panting, arrived. He greeted the Andersons, and seized Linda's arm firmly. "The car's halfway back to the club, but it couldn't be helped. Let's go. I don't believe we're late, at that," he said.

They were almost the last to arrive. In the cocktail lounge off the roof, Nelda greeted them, smiling, with Tony, looking very brushed, polished and proud, and her parents beside her. Linda had met the elder Herons on a prior occasion and liked them both, the big bluff man with the leonine head and the older, softer edi-

149

tion of Nelda who was Nelda's mother, her gold head turned prematurely platinum, but the fine skin as clear as her daughter's.

Dinner was lavish, and the guests were many, reminiscent of other days. There were souvenirs of the occasion: heart-shaped compacts for the women, with A.D. and N.H. reproduced across them in Nelda's small, square handwriting. There were cigarette holders for the men. The enormous table was banked with flowers and there was enough champagne, as Tom remarked, to launch a two-ocean navy.

Dancing with Tony, Linda asked, "Are you as happy as you look?"

"More so. Do you think an idiotic grin becomes me?" he inquired anxiously.

"Very much. Who's that dark man with the little beard who sat opposite me? I didn't catch his name."

"Dr. Benning . . . he's the big-shot psychiatrist," said Tony, "an old friend of the Herons'. He's alleged to have the best brainside manner in Manhattan."

Linda giggled. Tony was fun. He demanded, his arm tightening around her, "Having a good time, youngster?"

"Swell, but I wish it were Saturday night. I hate to stagger into the office tomorrow, all hung over," she said. "This sort of thing isn't good for the working woman. You know, Cinderella and all that. I'll wake up with my mind full of mice."

"Did you come with Tom?"

"Yep. Why?"

"Looks as if it was getting serious." He added, "I couldn't do anything about the Andersons. Nelda likes them a lot and so —"

"Don't bother," said Linda. She tilted her head to look up at him and her eyes were as clear as a child's. "I — well, I'm wholly over the hump, thanks to that sudden encounter at Heroncrest . . . and thanks to you too. It's all washed up, so don't give it another thought. Peg even came to see me the other afternoon, at the club. We're the best of friends," said Linda mendaciously.

He said, "I don't believe it."

"How discourteous. Them's fighting words. Why?"

"You're not the sort of girl who gets over things," he said, rather awkwardly, "I mean, as soon . . ."

"My dear Tony!" said Miss Wheaton tolerantly. "You haven't the remotest idea what sort of girl I am."

He looked down at her for a moment. "Maybe you're right," he said slowly.

"I decided," said Linda, "that carrying a torch didn't suit me. In the first place, too much heat and darned little light. I prefer fireflies, all light and no heat. I'm no blues singer," she told him, "and besides, I'm having too good a time. Whatever happened has happened, I can't undo it, but I can go on from there, can't I? I'd be silly not to — as staying in one place, marking time, gets you nowhere fast. Maybe you were right about one nail driving out another. Maybe what hurt me most was my pride —"

"And I don't believe that either," he said firmly.

"What a fruitless discussion," she murmured. "Skip it. I'm much more interested in you and your gal. And the music's stopping."

It was on the cards that she would dance with Rix before the evening was over. A week or so ago the thought of his arms about her — they had danced so much together, and beautifully — would have terrified her. Now she didn't mind. Not in the least. She told herself that firmly when she rose and looked at his smiling eyes. But some trepidation remained until his arms were close about her. She said to herself in astonishment, Why, I feel nothing, absolutely nothing. And it was true.

He asked, "Dare I say, this is like old times?"

"Well, not quite," she said, smiling.

He said, "Peg . . . she was out of turn, wasn't she, going to see you?"

"Why?" asked Linda. "We are more or less civilized, aren't we? — though sometimes, when I see the newspaper headlines, I doubt it."

"Linda, have you really forgiven me?" he asked soberly.

"In the sense you mean there was nothing to forgive, Rix," said Linda. "If I thought so for a time, it was my vanity speaking. You couldn't help falling in love with someone else. I don't think you were ever very much in love with me, now that I look back."

"But I was," he protested.

"You didn't know your own capacity," she said, smiling. "With us, it was just a question of did he fall or was he pushed. Pushed, I think, by propinquity, our families' intimacy, and the fact that from the time I was knee-high to a hoptoad, everyone thought of me as your girl. Suggestion, I think. Ask Dr. Benning about it."

"Who the heck is he?"

"A fellow guest," she said, "one of the medicos who deals with strange things like the power of suggestion and behavior patterns, to say nothing of conditioning and complexes. I danced with him a while back. He's very interesting. I'm busy planning a nervous breakdown, as he's very attractive as well."

"Linda, I don't give a damn about what's-his-name. If you knew how I felt when I saw you at Nelda's."

Did she imagine it or had his voice altered as he spoke Nelda's name?

"I know," she said, "I felt a little odd myself. But it's all over now. Meeting you, again, was the best thing that ever happened to me."

"Why?" he asked after a moment.

"Because it proved how utterly foolish I was, in being afraid that I might meet you. There's nothing like having what you fear most happen. Then there's nothing more to be afraid of, Rix, and you see how groundless your fears were all along. It's as if a child woke in the dark and saw an unknown shape and shrank from it. But when daylight comes he sees it's just a piece of furniture long familiar to him, and so not in the least frightening."

"What a flattering comparison," said Rix. "Look here, Linda."

"No," she said firmly. "Look at Tony and Nelda." They were dancing close to them and Nelda saw them, and smiled her slow, provocative smile and Tony beamed blissfully. But his eyes were a little anxious. Well, bless his heart, thought Linda, he's still worried about me.

She said aloud, as they lost Tony and his partner in the crowd, "They're such an attractive couple, don't you think?"

"Oh, sure," said Rix carelessly; "not that Tony's much to look at, but he's a good, sound guy."

"No," said Linda, "he isn't as handsome as Tom Yorke of course, nor you." She smiled at him, amused at his reaction. "You were always a little too good looking," she added critically, "which would have become a great anxiety to me after a while. It must be terrible to be compelled to compete with one's husband in, and for, the mirror."

"I like that!" said Rix, annoyed.

"Good," said Linda serenely. "But Peg can't have any such worry, as she's by far the prettiest woman at this party. She's even handsomer than Nelda . . . because her type lasts longer.

154

Blondes," stated Linda, "fade."

"You are a cat," said Rix. "By any chance, are you a little miffed because Tony Dennison is now judicially Nelda's?"

"Nope," said Linda, "I'm not. One thing for which I am grateful to you, Rix, is that you set up a sort of immunity in me."

"To — other men?" asked Rix, almost mechanically. This was the sort of line to which his responses were automatic.

"Wrong again. Not *other,* but all. Take it or leave it," she said. "Maybe it's rank flattery but I'm grateful just the same."

He said, "I don't know just how you mean that, Linda. Mother and Father are going to be in town next week. Somehow she's persuaded him to see me. If you — if you'd come to see them — have dinner with us at the flat or something, it would be generous of you, for it would help me a lot."

"I've just said I was grateful to you," she mused aloud. "Of course I'll come. Not that I care," she said frankly, "whether you and your father are reconciled or not, as far as you are concerned. But I care for your mother's sake. She doesn't deserve this situation, Rix. And she adores you. It hasn't been easy for her, I know. Tell Peg to call me up or send me a card or something and I'll turn up and convince them that everything's just dandy."

"I don't," he said cautiously, "like your tone."

She said, smiling, "Because it hurts your vanity

to think that I am all over it, doesn't it? Well, I can't help that, Rix, thank heaven."

He said, "Funny thing, I used to think that I knew you better than anyone in the world. And I went on thinking so, right up until I saw you again. Tonight, I'm more confused than ever."

"Confusion . . ." began Linda gravely. The music slid to a smooth sweet close, and they went back to their table.

Later, she saw him dancing with Nelda. He wasn't much taller than the girl, but tall enough. The dark head was close to the golden head. They waltzed perfectly together, with a lovely unity of step and fluid motion. Linda, with Dr. Benning sitting beside her, watched them and Benning said idly, "Now there's a rather ideal couple."

"Rix Anderson," she asked, "and Nelda?"

"Is that his name? Attractive young man," continued the doctor, "with a very beautiful wife who looks like a slumbering volcano."

"Yes," said Linda, "Peg does, rather." She added, "I've known them a long time."

"I've known Nelda since she was born," said Benning. "I'm old enough to be her father. There was a time when I wanted very much to marry her mother. I was a struggling young intern in those days and Heron came along, too soon." He smiled. "I'm Nelda's godfather, however," he went on, "and have always been fond of her. I very much hope that she will be happy in this proposed marriage."

Linda asked carefully, "You don't like Tony Dennison?"

Dr. Benning's bright dark eyes were thoughtful. He said, "My dear girl, I certainly did not mean to give you that erroneous impression. I like him enormously — the little I have seen of him. He's a very fine type . . . one of which this country can be proud, and which it will, one day, sacrifice for the good of the majority."

She asked, "Which means you think we'll get into this war?"

"I believe there's no doubt of it," he said gravely, "as the world has become something of a madhouse."

She said, "I — I don't like to think about it . . . but you were talking about Nelda, doctor."

He said, "Was I? Speculating aloud, perhaps. She needs a very firm hand on the reins, a hand almost ruthless. I doubt if young Dennison possesses the quality." He shrugged. "Still," he added, "I have made a wrong diagnosis before this and the emotion we term love is a marvelous thing . . . as unexpected as lightning from a blue sky, as uncertain as April weather, as incalculable as the woman who arouses it in a man." He smiled, "You're a very good listener." He went on, "And all men in my particular branch of the medical profession enjoy talking about themselves because so much of their work is spent in hearing others talk."

"You weren't talking about yourself," said Linda.

"Yes, I was. I was theorizing, a form of ego. I see that a redheaded gentleman is bearing down on us with blood in his eye. And the music has started."

Linda rose, smiled at Benning, and was taken into Tom Yorke's arms. He demanded, "What gives here? Were you getting a little psychoanalyzing free of charge? He looks like a guy who'd enjoy his work."

"Maybe I ought to consult him," said Linda, "except that I don't much want to know any more about myself than I do."

Later, in the powder room, she encountered Peg making a new mouth for herself and scowling into the mirror.

"Having a good time?" asked Linda, sitting down beside her.

"Rotten," said Peg. "Champagne makes my head ache."

Linda yawned. "It's late and I work for a living. I'll drag Tom away from Nelda's postdebutante pals and we'll get going."

"I'll stay here," said Peg viciously, "and watch Rix make a fool of himself. What else can I do?"

Linda powdered her nose. She commented, "I don't know why I bother. Put on your face, take it off, put it on again. Too silly. It's a wonder women have any skin left."

"You don't want to talk about Rix and Nelda," Peg accused her.

Linda swung around. "I don't want to talk about anyone when it's none of my business."

"Well, it's mine," said Peg. "I was dancing with someone — I don't even know the man's name. He was a little on the free-feeling side . . . a disgusting old boy, and we stood there politely clapping for the encore and he was asking for my telephone number . . . I bet he has a honey of an address book — and Rix and Nelda stood there too and didn't even look around and I heard him say, 'But you can't do this to me, Nelda, you can't.' And she said, 'I have to, Rix. Please trust me, it's the better way, it will be all right. Just be patient.' There's a word for that kind of woman," she said bitterly.

She met Linda's eyes in the glass, and flushed. She said, "I suppose you think there's a word for me too?"

"Several," said Linda mildly, "and one of them's idiot. You're unduly apprehensive, I think."

"Which is all you know about it."

Linda rose. She said, "I'll find Tom and demand to be taken home. Rix spoke to me about his parents' imminent arrival. I promised to be on deck when, and if, you want me and if you think it will help matters. I know you don't care especially. But Aunt Alice cares and she's the one I'm interested in, Peg. If it is possible for Rix and his father to be reconciled, then I'll do all I can, for his mother's sake."

"I can't see why . . ." began Peg.

"No," said Linda, "I suppose not. It's just that I find it more difficult than I thought to eradicate

Benfield and the old loyalties completely. Next to my mother I love Aunt Alice more than any woman in the world. And if you were wise, Peg, you'd be friends with her."

"Benfield isn't in my blood," said Peg.

"No," agreed Linda; "that's been quite apparent all along, hasn't it?"

Chapter 11

The Andersons came to New York and Linda kept her promise. It seemed fantastic to be here in Peg's apartment, which was very smart, very modern, with a costly address and view of the East River. But stranger still to sit at Peg's table and eat a passable dinner, passably served, and see beside her the familiar faces of Rix's mother and father. She regarded the scene and listened to the general conversation, which tried so hard not to be strained, with a curious detachment. Because it was incredible that less than a year ago she herself had planned such a dinner, one of many — only better, she informed herself, and how different a setting . . . with herself at the head of the table, in her own small, pretty house, the wedding presents shining new and bright, with Rix's parents to beam upon her and Rix in approval and Peg there, too, as a beloved guest and friend. But now Linda was the guest; hardly friend, and certainly not beloved.

Rix was too gay, and Peg too talkative. Aunt Alice tried too hard to make things seem natural, and easy; and Mr. Anderson, who didn't try at all, made them decidedly uncomfortable.

Linda escaped early. She made an engagement to dine with the Andersons, alone, at their hotel, and then pleaded work. "After all, I have a job," she said brightly, "and I've been keeping horrible hours."

"You look peaked," said Horace Anderson.

Rix insisted upon taking her home. It was absurd and put her in an unenviable position. If she should protest too much, she would leave an impression with his parents — if not with Peg as well — that she was afraid. But certainly she was quite capable of taking a bus across town and seeing herself safely to the club door.

In the end she had to permit the unwelcome attention and they went downstairs and the door-man called a taxi. In the cab, Rix broke the silence. "Mother looks all right, don't you think?" he inquired. "She's lost a little weight but that's to be expected the way she's working on all those relief committees. I wish they'd pack up and go south this year. The old man can afford the time and money but I don't suppose he will."

"No," agreed Linda, "it's not likely."

He said, "You were swell to come, it certainly helped matters. I hope to God that Peg quiets down . . . I mean, the way she rattles on."

"She was nervous," said Linda flatly.

"I suppose so, yet it's pretty silly. We're married and there's nothing anyone can do about it," he said, and was silent, throwing his cigarette to the taxi floor and stepping on it carefully.

Linda said, "Your mother is more than anxious to be friendly if Peg will just meet her halfway."

"Oh, she will," said Rix easily. "Linda, when

you see the folks again, will you try to persuade them that everything's all right and that it's a case of forgive and forget?"

"It should be simple," she said coolly, "as it happens to be perfectly true."

"Oh, sure," he said gloomily, "you never had any use for heels."

Linda drew a deep breath. "I'd have a lot more use for you, Rix, if you'd settle down and behave yourself."

"What does that mean, exactly?"

She said, "It hasn't escaped me that you and Nelda Heron are — well, let's say, entertaining yourselves, and at Peg's expense; to say nothing of Tony's."

"Peg's been complaining, I suppose?" he said. "Well, she's nuts."

"You can't dismiss it like that, and she hasn't complained," answered Linda, wondering why she bothered to lie for Peg. She didn't owe her that. "No, but I have eyes in my head."

"Very pretty ones," he said mechanically. "But you're crazy too."

"I hope so," Linda told him. "Not that I care whether Peg's hurt or not," she said calmly, "why should I? But I happen to like and admire Tony Dennison. Nelda's nothing to me and he's about a thousand times too good for her, as this little flutter proves. But Tony doesn't deserve to —"

"You're barking up the wrong tree," he interrupted. "Nelda's a very attractive girl, and I like her. But we're merely good friends. She has a line, and it's amusing. She knows all the answers. And I didn't forget them either just because I ceased to be a bachelor. We understand each other perfectly. There's nothing to it — nothing at all."

"I don't believe it," said Linda hotly, "and I'm beginning to understand you. Nelda's attractive, yes. Also, she has just slightly less than the gold at Fort Knox. So, if you hadn't been already married —"

"That's a different story," he retorted. "I was married, as it happened." He said something under his breath. Perhaps, "unfortunately."

"To fall heir to the Heron heiress," commented Linda, "would have been very comfortable. But as you say, you were married. And now Nelda's to be married. It's a pity that her parents are prejudiced against divorce; also they don't much like scandal, from what I hear. I'm warning you, Rix. If Mr. Heron has the least grounds for suspicion, he can make things unpleasant for you — in your job and otherwise — and then where will you be?"

"There's always Benfield," he answered, and laughed.

"I wonder?" said Linda. "Back to the bank? Even if your father was willing, it might not be as easy for you, or for Peg, as you think. People have long memories in New England; and they are loyal."

He said sharply:

"Linda, we were once in love with each other.

As you say, you've recovered and so have I. I hoped we could be friends. We were once, you know. But this little conversation isn't proving very helpful — or friendly."

"In other words," she asked, "I'm to mind my own business?"

"If you want to put it that way," Rix agreed. "I'm no longer any concern of yours; nor is Peg. You've as much as said so. And Nelda isn't, by your own admission. Also, I doubt if Dennison would thank you for interfering, although he's the one of us all who seems to cause you anxiety. He's in love with Nelda and he wouldn't be grateful if you tried to make trouble between him and Nelda."

"I make trouble?" Linda laughed. "You're impossible, Rix, and I should have known it."

"Naturally," he agreed, "by now."

The cab stopped, they had reached the club. "Thank you," said Linda, getting out, "for a most enlightening evening."

Enlightening it was. His denial had carried no weight. His counterwarning was clear enough. Stay out of this. I'll do as I damned please without regard for Dennison *or* my wife.

Cynthia came out of the lounge as Linda entered the club. "You look plenty abstracted. And you're home early," she remarked.

"That sounds as if I staggered in every morning at six," said Linda, smiling. "I was abstracted. I was pondering on the vagaries of human nature."

"Which will get you nowhere," said Cynthia,

"as none of us is competent to judge, being prone to vagaries ourselves."

Linda said good night and went on upstairs. She thought, Cynthia's sensible and sound. I'd like to talk to her. But I can't. I don't want intimacies. Whatever I do from now on is my own affair.

She had dined with the Andersons in the dining room of their big hotel and later went back to their rooms with them to talk of her mother and father, and Benfield in general. Horace Anderson excused himself after a while. He was tired, he said, New York had worn him to a frazzle, he was going to bed. "You see," said Alice Anderson, running her hands through her thick white hair, "he's so afraid one of us will say something. He won't discuss the situation. He has accepted it, because he has to. But he hasn't forgiven Rix."

Linda said, "I wish he would. I have." She smiled at the older woman. "Darling, don't look so bothered. It's really all right and quite all over. I'm fine."

"I wish I could believe that, Linda. You're such a strong little thing. And you hate hurting people."

There must be some way to convince her, to send her back to Benfield easier in her mind, lighter in heart.

"I've a confession to make. You won't tell anyone? Not even Mother and Father?" Linda asked.

"Of course not. What is it, Linda?"

"Just that — there's someone else."

Alice looked incredulous and aghast. "There couldn't be — so soon."

What a reputation I have, thought Linda, for bulldog tenacity. Old last-ditch Wheaton, that's me. Tony thinks so; and now Aunt Alice. I believe, she thought further, both irritated and amused, she's disappointed in me. No matter what Rix has done, she can't understand anyone who'd once been in love with him getting over it.

She shook her head at Alice, smiling. "But there is," she said, "so you see, as far as last winter is concerned, you needn't worry."

Alice said, "Linda dear, I'm so glad." She was, her face showed it, the brown eyes luminous. And yet, Linda thought, poor darling, she'll always be a little hurt. She does want me to be happy, but she wants almost as much to believe in the legend of Rix the irresistible, the ungetoverable. "Is — is he anyone I know?" Alice asked.

"I can't tell you," said Linda, "because he isn't aware of it yet although I'm working on him," she said, smiling. "And you'll have to let it go at that. But please believe me."

You, my girl, she told herself, slightly appalled, are becoming an accomplished liar.

"May I tell Horace?"

"If you wish. But no one else. You know," said Linda coaxingly, "it would upset Mother and

Father dreadfully if they found out I'd told anyone else — even you — first. I wouldn't have
said a word," she added veraciously, "if I hadn't
known you were still worried about me."

Alice's eyes rested on the small cluster of tiny
yellow orchids which decorated the shoulder of
Linda's blue linen suit. She asked slowly, "Didn't
Rix tease you at dinner the other night about
someone named Yorke?"

"Check," said Linda, "and the orchids are
from him, Philo Vance." She laughed. "But don't
go getting any ideas," she warned. Still, this was
as good an idea as any, she thought.

"Linda," asked Mrs. Anderson abruptly, "do
you think Rix and Peg are happy?"

"Of course," said Linda, a little too swiftly.

"I'm not at all sure," began Alice, "and I can't
explain why, but there's something wrong there.
I can't put my finger on it."

"Nonsense," said Linda briskly, "it was the
situation, that's all. Rix knows how his father
feels and he's ashamed at having hurt him, and
you. Peg feels that way too, so it's natural that
things should be a little strained at first."

"I asked them to come home this summer if
Rix took a vacation," said Alice slowly, "but they
didn't promise."

"Well," said Linda lightly, "it's better to let a
little more water run under the Main Street
bridge, don't you think? I've refused to go home
too. Maybe in the autumn, but I don't know.
Mother and Father said they'd come down here,

and we might take a little trip together, not that I rate a vacation but Mr. Powell is very good to me. We'll see." She leaned forward to put her hand on Mrs. Anderson's. "Cross me off your list of worries, Aunt Alice. I've never felt better in all my life."

"You're too thin," said Mrs. Anderson absently. And there was something else, evasion, wariness, under a brittle manner, not exactly hard but certainly entirely new, which disturbed her in Linda, although she could not put it into words. She said, sighing, "It's — I just want you to be happy, Linda. And Rix." She added with an obvious effort, "And, of course, Peg."

The summer days went past, flawless blue skies, brazen sun, the asphalt soft under feet loath to hurry. The law offices were air conditioned. When she was working there Linda forgot the heat and when she left in the afternoon and reached the crowded streets the temperature struck her like a blow, the humidity left her dripping. She joined the YWCA and, with Cynthia and others, went swimming evenings in the big pool. She did not see Rix nor Peg, and Tony Dennison was often out of town. Tom Yorke took her often to a cool rooftop for dinner and dancing, and on several Sundays she drove out of town with him to Westchester or Connecticut to some inn by a pond or on a lake or, on the Island, by the sea. He spent most of his weekends in Southampton, however, and more than once suggested that she accept the formal and open invitation of his mother to accompany him. But Linda refused. She had met Tom's family by now, including his formidable great-aunt, and liked them well enough, but it was obvious that they were regarding her in the light of a possibly prospective daughter-in-law and, as such, she would be more or less on trial. As she had no intention of filling this difficult bill she was not anxious to be put in a position of accepting their on-approval hospitality.

Toward the end of August, however, she went to the Herons'. Nelda had written her several times, asking her to come down for this weekend or that but Linda had always managed to get out of it. Occasionally Nelda came to town and picked up Tony at the office for luncheon and each time she had invaded Linda's anteroom and filled her with the despair natural to the woman who feels herself at a disadvantage. Linda always felt as if her hair was in strings, her powder sticky and her face smudged with carbon and probably bright red when Nelda strolled in, dressed for town in something dark and sheer, devastatingly becoming, cooler than a frozen Daiquiri and perfectly unruffled from head to foot, her clear pale skin, its flawless ivory unaffected by sun, wind or temperature.

Finally, there was no getting out of it. Tony argued with her for an entire week. "If you don't," he said, "I'll begin to think you don't like us. Honestly, Linda, it will do you good, sun and air and the sea. You won't be run ragged, I promise you that. We'll let you rest" — he grinned at her — "although I don't know about Tom. He'll be around, you know."

He looked at her. "As a favor to me," he said, "come on, Linda. Give."

So late one Friday afternoon Linda drove down with Tony to the house set back from the dunes and ocean, a gray frame structure, with two big wings, and gardens, and land which ran to the sea. She was, she admitted, breathing the salt air, more tired than she had thought with the heat of town. It was good to be out of it, away from the noise and traffic, the dispirited papers whirling in dusty gutters, the sound of radios and the ceaseless tension of a big city under humid, blanketing heat.

Nelda seemed glad to see her. The Prestons were there and Mr. and Mrs. Heron. The house ran smoothly, and house guests did as they pleased. Breakfast in bed, a swim before, if you liked, golf or tennis for anyone who wished, or simply lying on the terrace or under the umbrellas on the private beach. For fun, and people, if you wanted them, you went to the club, and you went other places for cocktails or dinner or dancing.

Tom turned up the following morning and spent it on the Heron beach under a striped umbrella, arguing with Linda that the Yorkes were as good as the Herons any day in the week, not to mention the weekend, so what was the idea of turning down their invitations?

Linda, observing Tony and Nelda, became gradually aware that things were not running too smoothly. She couldn't say why she knew this. Nelda's treatment of her fiancé was a little casual, perhaps, but then Nelda was always casual. But Tony had lost the crazy, don't-care-who-knows-it happiness of the early days of their engagement and more than once Linda came upon them, if not quarreling then, at least, in a deep, not too pleasant discussion. She believed she knew what was back of the change when, on Saturday afternoon, Rix Anderson arrived alone, and prepared to spend the night.

That he was not particularly pleased to see Linda was obvious when she came downstairs, after a nap, at cocktail time and found him there. But his first, disconcerted expression quickly altered to the easy warmth of pleasure. "Swell seeing you," he said, "Nelda didn't tell me when I phoned her and asked if I might barge in." He explained further. "Peg's in Westchester with some old California friends and I had to see a man about a million dollars in Easthampton. I spent last night there and today, but couldn't contemplate the apartment tonight, hot and empty. I don't happen to like Peg's native son pals, so here I am, intruding as usual."

Nelda, Linda perceived at once, had come to life since Rix's arrival. Oh, not too obviously, of course, but if you were looking for a sign there it was. It was also evident, at least to Linda, that

Tony had as yet no suspicion. He was cordial to Rix, and Tony was no hypocrite, it wasn't in him to be cordial to anyone he disliked or suspected; courteous, yes, but not cordial. Whatever had happened between himself and Nelda, he hadn't the remotest idea that Rix was connected with it, if, indeed, he was, Linda thought, wondering if much of this was her unbridled imagination.

That evening they all went over to Canoe Place to dance and have supper. Tom Yorke was with them, Rix was the extra man, so Nelda had enlisted a small, provocative blonde in the cause.

Driving back, Linda was with Tom, alone in his car, and they reached the Heron house after the others because he pulled off the road and parked, in order to give her, he said, a view of the bay, and despite her protests they remained there for some time.

"It's no use, Linda," he said, "I'm a gone gander. The game's up. For you, I will become a benedict, much as it terrifies me. I think," he added, more seriously than she had ever heard him speak, "that we could make a good life together. We laugh at the same things, we have fun, and despite income taxes and such mundane considerations I could buy jam for your croissants. I'm a pretty good lawyer, I expect to be a better one, and as a member of the firm I draw more than I earn. In addition —"

She knew. The Yorkes had plenty of money. They were not in the Heron class, but they weren't likely to go hungry.

"Tom —"

"Oh, don't say it," he begged her, "give a guy a chance. I'm very much in love with you, Linda." He pulled her toward him, kissed her squarely on the mouth. "There," he said, releasing her. "Was it so dreadful?"

"No," she told him, "it was rather nice." It was. She had had a number of opportunities to be kissed since her arrival in New York but had until now evaded them all, including Tom's tentative attempts. She thought, It is pleasant, I like him, he's attractive, it would be awfully easy to drift into this sort of thing, with no chart, no compass to tell you where you're heading.

"Then," he asked happily, "I don't exactly revolt you?"

"Not exactly," she admitted, laughing.

He took her in his arms again. "Then," he demanded, "what are we waiting for? Let's go back and break the news. Me, an engaged man!" he added in astonishment. "I can't believe it."

"You needn't," she said, "because you aren't. Of course, the White Queen believed seven — was it seven? — impossible things before breakfast, but this isn't before breakfast."

"Yes, it is," he argued, "it's nearer before breakfast than after dinner."

"You aren't the White Queen," she told him, "and if this is an oblique way of asking my hand in marriage, Mr. Yorke, the answer is No."

"But why?" he asked plaintively.

"Silly of me, isn't it?" she asked lightly. "But I'm not in love with you."

He said, in relief, "Is that all? You will be. Can't we announce it first and fall in love after? You, I mean."

"Benfield," Linda said, "never puts the cart before the horse. Let's go back now, Tom."

"Mad?"

"No," she answered; "flattered. And I do like you very much. You are a nice person and fun. But —"

He said hopefully, "It's a step in the right direction. Mind if I kiss you again?"

"Not at all," said Linda, "but it mustn't become a habit. Just on very special occasions, like this one."

This time she drew away from his embrace, more shaken than she cared to admit to herself. It's loneliness, she decided, and a sort of salve to hurt pride. It was like that night at home coming back from the movies with Fred. Well, not quite.

She said, "I'm sorry, Tom, there mustn't be any more special occasions. I've changed my mind."

"Why?" he asked. "You're the damnedest girl!"

She said, "I was trying to be honest with you. I liked that, rather a lot. I don't want to. I don't want to be kissed just because I can enjoy having a personable man kiss me. It isn't good enough, Tom."

"Okay," he said, "I see your point. But I shan't give up trying — perhaps if you are exposed enough to being loved you'll catch the disease."

They drove back in silence and he left her at the Heron house, where a sleepy but resigned butler let her in. Miss Nelda and the others, he told her with veiled reproach, had reached home some time ago and gone up to their rooms.

Linda went to hers, which overlooked the gardens. There was moonlight on white flowers, on the sand beyond and the stretch of sea visible from her windows, open to the coolness and quiet of the night, to the restless sighing of the sea and the scent of flowers growing. She undressed, turned out the lights, belted a thin silk robe about her and went out on the little balcony which ran outside her windows and sat down in a low chair to smoke a cigarette and think. She was sorry about tonight. She wished it had not happened. It had taught her a little too much about herself and frightened her. She thought, I mustn't see as much of Tom, it isn't fair to him and it would be down-right stupid of me.

After a time she heard a murmur of voices under the windows and rose to look over the balcony railing. There was a faint light from somewhere, the hall perhaps, and she could see Nelda, as there was no mistaking her height and carriage, and also the man with her. Rix, of course; Tony and Tom were both taller. They stopped for a moment directly beneath her. If she moved now they would know she was there and she had no wish to be found, an unwilling eavesdropper. She had put out the cigarette a moment before, so the light did not betray her. She wanted to put her fingers in her ears and close her eyes but she couldn't. She thought, I have to know.

She heard Nelda speak in a voice she had not heard her use before, yet the word she uttered was one often on her lips, but this time with a difference. "Darling," she said.

She was close in Rix's arms. Linda heard only one thing that he said, and it was enough. He said, "I won't give you up, no matter what happens. You're crazy to go through with this, Nelda, but I won't give you up."

"You don't have to," Nelda said.

They kissed again for a long, mindless moment and then turned away. Linda went back to her room, after a while. She took off the robe and threw herself across the bed. She thought, It isn't fair, it's horrible. She thought of Tony and her heart was wrung for him. If Nelda broke it off, so much the better for him in the long run. It would be the clean, the decent way. But Nelda wouldn't, nor would Rix try to force her to. That wasn't his way. History could, obliquely, repeat itself. And Linda thought, Someone has to do something about this. Someone has to ask her if she intends to marry Tony and carry on this affair with Rix. And there's no one but me, she thought, frightened and sick.

After a while she rose, put her robe on again, found her slippers in the dark, and went softly out of the room to Nelda's.

Chapter 12

The wide corridor was silent. A shaded light shone softly. The heels of Linda's mules tick-tacked along the polished floor. She held her breath lest a door open and someone, Mrs. Heron perhaps or, worse, Tony, look out to see who crept along the hall at this hour of the night. She knew which was Nelda's room, as she had been in and out of it several times since yesterday, but was afraid that, in her nervousness, she might mistake the door. All these doors looked alike, the shining white panels closed against intrusion. Why am I doing this? she asked herself, halting before a door. It's none of my business what Nelda does . . . or what happens to Tony, because she does it. I must be out of my mind.

Her heart beat quickly, the blood pounded in her temples, the palms of her hands were cold and wet, and little shivers of apprehension ran along her spine. She hesitated, her hand upraised to knock, and then half turned away. It was not too late, she had not committed herself, she could go back as silently as she had come. If anyone chanced to see her, she could say she had a headache and had gone to Nelda's room to beg an aspirin, and had then changed her mind, disliking to awaken her hostess.

No, Tony was too decent, she reminded herself fiercely, to have a thing like this happen to him. When he found out — and he was bound to find out, for you had been taught, in Benfield, that people are always found out — he was certain to be badly hurt. And if he didn't find out until after he and Nelda were married, how immeasurably, irrevocably worse.

She drew a deep breath, steadied the shaking of her traitor hands and knees, and knocked. She knocked twice, softly, before she heard someone stirring inside and Nelda's voice asking, "Who is it?"

"Linda."

Nelda opened the door and regarded her with smiling inquiry. She was not yet ready for bed. She wore a wisp of black chiffon and lace, and her heavy, dull-gold hair streamed over her shoulders. Her eyes were bright and drowsy, and her mouth wore the soft, vulnerable look of a woman who has recently been kissed and not against her will. Her lipstick had been wiped off and her lips were pink. She held a jar of cold cream in her hand.

"Linda, is anything the matter?" she asked, astonished.

There was one way out. Take it. Say, I had such a crashing headache that I couldn't sleep. I'm so sorry to disturb you . . . but have you aspirin? — easy, disarming. A way she couldn't take.

Linda said, "No . . . that is . . . may I come

180

in and talk to you, Nelda?"

"Why, of course." Nelda smiled but her eyes were startled, and curious. "As you see, I hadn't gone to bed. I was reading." Now the door closed behind Linda and she was in the room which had been decorated to hold Nelda's beauty . . . a room like a jewel box, all pastel pinks and blues, muted greens. It was large, there was a four-poster, canopied bed, a chaise longue, a French powder table glistening with crystal, silver, enamel.

"Sit down," said Nelda. "Mind if I go on with the usual nonsense? Cigarettes there at your elbow. What happened to you and Tom, tonight?"

Linda sat down in a low chair. She did not want to smoke. Nelda sat at the dressing table, her back to Linda. She pinned her heavy hair back, bound a white towel about her head and was instantly transformed. Her face had a classic loveliness, the cheekbones prominent, the chin pointed, the eyebrows like brown satin wings. She dipped her long, redtipped fingers into the squat jar, and slowly creamed her face with long, upward movements. She moistened a pad of cotton in a clear liquid from a crystal bottle.

Linda could see Nelda's face in the mirror. She could watch it. She waited, weighing her words, and Nelda laughed. She asked, "Is your New England conscience bothering you? Tony was as fretful as a cat. 'What in heaven's name has happened to Linda and Tom?' he kept asking. 'Do you suppose there's been an accident?' I told

181

him you'd probably taken the long way home."
She smiled at Linda and even the shining cream
could not disfigure her. She washed it off with
the lotion and dipped her fingers into another jar
and dotted more cream over her face. She picked
up a little rubber patter from the dressing table
and holding it by the plastic handle, began to
drum it lightly along her jaw line, over cheekbones, under eyes.

She said, "Blondes sag, you know," in an
explanatory fashion.

Linda found her voice and words. She said,
"Tom and I parked awhile and watched the bay."

"A perfectly reasonable explanation," said
Nelda calmly. The corners of her mouth twitched
with amusement, "You're doing pretty well for
yourself, unless signs fail," she said, "and if you
believe in signs."

Linda ignored that. She said slowly, "You and
Tony came home before us, with the Prestons
and Rix."

"Of course. We dropped Nancy at her house
first," Nelda said.

"You went out again," said Linda.

Nelda's reflected face was expressionless. The
soft drumming went on. She asked after a moment, "What do you mean, I went out?"

Linda spoke evenly. Her heart had quieted.
She had made up her mind. She would go
through with this, however distasteful. She answered:

"You, and Rix, forgot when you came back

182

from the — beach, perhaps, or the garden, that my windows were directly . . ." She paused and added, "I happened to be on the balcony."

"Oh," said Nelda. She put down the patter and swung around on the dressing table bench. Her clean, shining face had great purity of line under the severe headdress of the towel. She asked, "And what do you intend to do about it?"

Her long, slender body shone, ivory white, through the inadequate veiling of black chiffon. Her eyes were wary but untroubled, her face imperturbable, but Linda could see the long breath she drew, flattening her ribs, held a moment and then expelled.

She said quietly, "I don't think that's the point. I think the point is, what do you intend to do?"

"I," said Nelda, "intend to do as I please."

"Which means both Rix and Tony please you?"

Nelda smiled. She said gently, "I don't know why you take such an interest in my affairs, Linda. It's flattering, but incomprehensible."

Linda said sturdily, "Tony's my friend."

"He happens to be engaged to me," Nelda reminded her.

"And Rix — who isn't?"

"I find Rix very amusing."

"Was tonight — under my window — your idea of amusement? It wouldn't be Tony's," said Linda. Anger was hot in her veins, contempt cooled it.

Nelda looked directly into the blazing blue

eyes. She said, "It seems to me that you are going to a good deal of trouble for — a friend, however devoted. And putting yourself at the same time in a questionable position."

"In other words, I'm to mind my own business?"

"That sounds very rude," said Nelda, considering. "But, well, yes. Definitely."

"Suppose I make it my business?" asked Linda.

"What, exactly, can you do?" Nelda inquired. "Go to Tony, tell him that you were present, as an invisible audience, shall we say, tonight when Rix and I played out our little scene under your windows? And what will that amount to? Your word against mine. I can deny it. Which of us is Tony apt to believe? I'm sure he'd rather believe me."

Linda said, "He's in love with you, Nelda. He would want to believe you with all his heart and soul. But he knows that I don't lie."

"How quaint," commented Nelda. "Never? You should be in a museum. But I still don't see what you gain or why you —"

Linda interrupted, with slow fury. "I won't have Tony hurt," she said.

"So that's it," said Nelda. "Sacrificial and noble. You won't have Tony hurt! You must be very fond of him, Linda. A beautiful friendship." She looked at her and laughed. "Are you by any chance trying to throw a monkey wrench," she inquired, "for purposes of your own?"

For a moment Linda said nothing. She returned Nelda's regard steadily. Then she said, "Suppose we don't talk about Tony, Nelda. Suppose, instead, we talk about Rix?"

"Don't tell me," said Nelda, "that just because you were brought up together you have constituted yourself Rix's guardian too. You do carry friendship to remarkable lengths."

"Is that all Rix told you about me," said Linda, "that we were brought up together?"

Nelda stirred uneasily. "My dear girl, what else is there to tell?" she answered.

"Rix and I," said Linda quietly, "were to be married. We'd been engaged a long time. We were to have been married last January. Our plans were made, our house —" She stopped. She had done no harder thing than this. "My trousseau was ready. He and Peg eloped shortly before what was to have been my wedding day."

Nelda's fair skin darkened with sudden blood. She said flatly, "I don't believe it."

"I doubt if Rix would deny it," said Linda steadily, "as Peg wouldn't. Peg, you know, hasn't been blind to your interest in him or to his in you. And if you don't care to ask her — or him, why not ask Tony? He knew. He was in Benfield last October. He met me then, and Rix, and knew of our engagement. He met Peg too. He sent me, by the way, a very attractive present which, naturally, I returned."

"So that accounts for it," Nelda said slowly.
"For what?"
"For Tony's attitude when he met the Ander-

sons at my house; and also, for the very strange atmosphere which didn't escape me when you met them. But I don't understand why Tony didn't tell me."

"Why should he?" inquired Linda. "You weren't engaged to him at the time. He isn't a gossip. My position was sufficiently uncomfortable, as it was, without having it broadcast."

"It must have been very embarrassing to encounter the man who jilted you, Linda," Nelda said.

"Yes," Linda agreed evenly, "it was. And for him too, and Peg."

"Peg," said Nelda astonishingly, "can hardly complain about me!"

"That's an odd viewpoint," Linda told her. "But as far as that goes, I am not interested in Peg's reactions."

Nelda said, "My dear, there's no point in this conversation, interesting though it may be. Because your motive is so very clear."

"Just what," asked Linda, "is my motive?"

"You," said Nelda, "are jealous. Of Rix, perhaps . . . perhaps you're still in love with him. Or is it because of Tony? I wouldn't know."

Linda said, "I don't care what you know or what you think. I am merely warning you."

"Warning me," Nelda repeated, and raised an eyebrow.

"Yes. Peg isn't a complacent wife. She is very much in love with Rix. If she creates a scandal — and she is perfectly capable of it — your parents won't like it. Tony won't either. And you won't be able to talk yourself out of it."

"Peg," said Nelda disdainfully, and dismissed Rix's wife with a shrug. "Just what has she to go on, unless, of course, you intend to tell her what you imagine you saw. And naturally both Rix and I will deny that you saw anything."

She was right, of course. Peg had little evidence upon which to convict her husband or Nelda Heron. Suspicion, yes . . . and an insane jealousy which could magnify a word, a look. Linda shook her head. She said, "I have no intention of going to Peg — or to anyone but you. Nelda, I don't know what you intend to do but —"

"I intend," interrupted Nelda, "to do just as I said, which is as I please. I intend to marry Tony. I'm fond of him, it will be a much better marriage than most."

"You'll have your cake and eat it too?"

"An absurd saying," Nelda commented. "If you eat your cake, naturally you have it. If you have it you don't put it on the mantelpiece as decoration, you eat it." She smiled again. "I don't want you to think I'm annoyed or angry," she said, "I understand perfectly. It's one of two things with you, Linda: you're still in love with Rix or you want to get even with him, if you can, for what he did to you. Or else you've decided, just as I did, that Tony would make a good settled sort of husband. He has position, and from your viewpoint, enough money. A good marriage would be nice for you, wouldn't it? It would make the people back in — what's the name of the town? — forget. Or perhaps you have fallen in love with him on the rebound. That must be it," she concluded with decision, "otherwise you'd take Tom Yorke. *If* he's serious about you. Which, somehow or other, I doubt."

Linda asked, "Nelda, haven't you any decency?"

"Our ideas on decency may differ."

"I'm sure they do," said Linda. "You're only laying up trouble for yourself and hurt for Tony, and trying to break up a marriage as well. Why? You don't want to marry Rix, do you?"

"Certainly not," said Nelda, "I'm not a fool."

"Then what *do* you want?"

"Suppose I say I'm in love with him," Nelda said, "in a way you could not understand? I'll get over it. But I'm in no hurry. And until I do —"

"Rix isn't in love with you," said Linda, "nor with anyone except himself. He always thinks he is . . . at the time. He thought he was, with me. He thought he was, with Peg. And now, with you. But you are bigger game than I was, or Peg. I was just a girl he'd always known, and Peg was someone new, and exciting and exotic. But you are Nelda Heron. Can't you see what he's trying to do? He's willing to let you break up his marriage, openly enough, hoping Peg will eventually divorce him, and that there will be sufficient scandal to force you to marry him, regardless of your own wishes or what your parents say. He'd never believe that they'd disinherit you . . . he'd believe that, in due time, their love for you and his own ingratiating charm would cause them to forgive and forget. Happy ending," said Linda bitterly, "for Rix at least."

Nelda's ivory pallor was gray. She said, "I think you've said quite enough. You've warned me. Well, I warn you. If you say a word of this to Tony or to Peg Anderson, I'll swear it is not true, not a word of it. I'll say you're jealous. I'll tell Tony that I forced you to admit you were in love with him and would stop at nothing to break our engagement."

Linda rose and went to the door. She said, "All right, Nelda. Play it your own way. I had no intention of going to Tony or Peg. I came to headquarters instead. To you. Because you're the only person who can remedy this. But you wouldn't, of course. You're completely egotistical and amoral. I'll leave," she went on quietly, "in the morning. I'll make some excuse. There must be a train I can take. It would be awkward for us both if I were to remain until evening, as we'd planned, and drove back with Tony."

"You can do as you please," Nelda flung at her.

Linda closed the door. She was out in the corridor and now she was shaking again. She was sick with frustration and fatigue. What a fool she had been to think Nelda would listen to her, would not plot and plan to twist the situation to her own advantage! That's what I get for meddling, she told herself, going softly to her own room, and locking herself in. The Girl Scout instinct. The good deed. A fine deed *that* turned out to be!

Well, this was the end of her acquaintance with the sacrosanct Herons, she thought. She was dead tired but completely wide awake. She took out her suitcase and began to pack. She would get up early, ring, do the necessary tipping, and ask the butler to call a taxi for her, saying she didn't wish to disturb Miss Heron or her parents at that hour. She would leave the usual apologetic note, saying she had had an urgent telephone call and must return at once to town. No one was likely to check on the excuse, certainly Nelda wouldn't.

Well, where was she? Just where she was before, or a couple of miles in the rear. Nelda wouldn't stop seeing Rix; she would marry Tony; she would do as she pleased. She had said so. And now she knew all about Rix and Linda and Peg, and didn't care. The knowledge merely provided her with a weapon. Linda could imagine vividly all Nelda would or could say to Tony . . . not in her own defense, which would be unnecessary, but to discredit Linda in his eyes, to make it very plausible why the Herons no longer asked Tony's little friend, Mr. Powell's secretary, to their various houses.

"Of course, darling," she would say, "she's still in love with Rix Anderson. It doesn't matter to her that he's married someone else. Why, last time she was visiting us I saw with my own eyes . . ."

She'd keep Rix in the clear, of course. "Poor dear, he was terribly upset. You could have knocked me over with a zombie when I discovered they'd once been engaged."

Or, and still worse — "Haven't you guessed that Linda's crazy about you, Tony?"

It would need only that to embarrass Tony to the point of extreme discomfiture. Contrary to a general impression, men do not enjoy being informed that some girl, for whom they care not at all, is carrying a bright torch for them. It may flatter them for the time being but, whether or not their affections are otherwise engaged, it embarrasses them too. And if their affections are engaged, so much the worse.

Nelda had only to say that, and to point it up with evidence which she could easily manufacture. Tony would be incredulous, he would laugh it off, but he wouldn't forget. He would cease to be natural with Linda and gradually, because the idea — whether mistaken or not on Nelda's part — made him uncomfortable, he would avoid her.

And the stupid part, thought Linda, cramming clothes recklessly into the suitcase, is that I was trying to help him . . . trying to save him, if I could, from being hurt. Perhaps this will teach me to mind my own business, as Nelda, and Rix, before her, had suggested.

She went to bed and lay sleepless. There was not much left of that miserable Saturday night.

When it grew light she rose and dressed and when she thought the servants would be stirring, she rang. An astonished and rather reproachful maid knocked at her door and Linda told her to come in. She explained, smiling, "I'm so sorry . . . but I learned late last night that I had to return to town on the first train. I wonder if I could get a taxi? I don't want to disturb anyone, I'll leave a note for Miss Heron. But if you could get me a timetable?"

She put a bill in the maid's hand and the girl brightened to attention. She said, "I'll ask Blower —" Blower, it seemed, was the butler, a wonderful name, thought Linda abstractedly — "he has a timetable. And I'll bring you your coffee at once, miss."

Linda said hastily that coffee was not necessary. But the girl hurried away and presently returned with a tray, coffee, orange juice, toast, marmalade, and the timetable. "Blower says," she reported, "that there isn't a train Sunday morning. The early one runs on weekdays. It's seven something."

Linda's heart sank. "Thanks," she said, "I'll see if I can get a taxi to take me into town."

It would cost a fortune, she thought, if she could get someone to drive her, and even that wasn't certain.

She heard a telephone ring as she sat there on a chair by the window and drank the coffee. She thought, Tom, I could call him and ask him if he'd drive me up at once; of course he would, he probably has all sorts of plans for today but he'd drop them and drive me in. And I don't want to ask him.

It would be a last resort. She couldn't stay here. She had to get away, she couldn't remain under the same roof with Nelda another hour, under the obligation of Heron hospitality. Even the coffee seemed bitter. She thought, If I can't get a taxi to take me in, I'll have to call Tom and tell him it's life or death.

She heard Blower come upstairs and knock at a door. You couldn't mistake the stately footsteps. She heard a man's sleepy voice answering. Rix. The telephone call was for Rix. A little later she heard him go down the hall.

She rose, went to a mirror and pulled her little hat over one bright blue eye. She sat down at the desk and wrote the note to Nelda. The so-sorry-but-called-away note which the elder Herons, which Tony and Rix or anyone literate, could read without speculation. She addressed and sealed it, and put it in her handbag. She would give it to Blower. When Rix had finished talking, when she heard him come upstairs and go in his room and shut the door, she would take her suitcase and go downstairs to ask to use the telephone, to call, first a taxi and then, if necessary, Tom.

She heard Rix return but his hurrying feet did not stop at his door, passed on and stopped at hers and he knocked. "Linda," he called, "let me in."

Chapter 13

Startled, Linda opened the door. Rix stood there, a bathrobe flung over his pajamas, his dark hair tousled, his face very white. He said, "You're dressed . . . good," as if there was nothing unusual in her being ready to leave this house at this hour in the morning. "It's Peg," he said, "I —"

He shook, and Linda put her hand on his arm. She warned, "You'll waken everyone, Rix. Come in, sit down. Tell me what has happened. What about Peg?"

"They called me up," he said, "from Westchester. The Weldons, that is, Peg's friends, with whom she was spending the weekend. It seems that she went to bed early last night, said she didn't feel well, and Gwen Weldon went into her room just a few minutes ago to see how she was. They'd heard her crying earlier, last night, but she wouldn't let Gwen in then. Anyway, she isn't there. The bed hadn't been slept in. Sometime in the night she'd gone. They said they went to bed early, about eleven. Peg had gone up about nine. Gwen said it was about eleven when they heard her crying and knocked. Peg said to go away, she was all right. But some time later — after they were asleep

194

— she left. She dressed and went away," said Rix, "but she left her suitcase there and just took her handbag."

"But that's —" Linda stopped. Left her suitcase, she thought, but why? Did she intend to return?

She said, "Look, Rix, you're upset over nothing. Perhaps Peg didn't go out until early this morning and then just for a walk."

"Then why isn't she back?" asked Rix. "I've got to go up there. I've got to find out. Linda," he said, like a child, "please come with me."

That was habit, she told herself. Up until not very long ago he had turned to her for everything: when he got in a jam, if his father was displeased with him . . .

"All right, Rix," she said. "Go and dress and I'll get Blower to get you some coffee."

Rix went to the door, then turned. He said helplessly, "I can't understand it. Peg just doesn't do things like that. If she'd decided to return to New York she would have told Gwen, and why did she leave her suitcase?"

"Listen," said Linda soothingly, "we'll telephone, along the way. You'll probably find that she's already returned, and that it's a tempest in a teapot."

He looked at her as if he saw her for the first time. His eyes went to the suitcase. He asked, "You — you were leaving?"

"I found I had to get back," she said. "It doesn't matter now, what I had to do will keep.

I didn't want to bother anyone. Do go get dressed, Rix."

He left her door open as he went into the corridor and Linda, trying to reorganize her thoughts, had picked up her suitcase and started for the door when Nelda appeared, wrapped in a sea-green negligee, her eyes wide and suspicious. "Where are you going, you and Rix?" she demanded. "I heard him at your door. What's going on here?"

Linda said coolly, "I was leaving." She took the note from her handbag and laid it on the dresser. "My alibi," she explained. "Unfortunately there isn't an early train. I was going to get a taxi to take me to town or, failing that, telephone Tom Yorke, when Rix came to tell me he had had a call from the people whom Peg's been visiting in Westchester — apparently she's disappeared."

Nelda's face sharpened, she looked old in that moment, and frightened. "Disappeared?" she repeated shrilly.

"That's what they told Rix," said Linda.

"But, how absurd." Nelda tried to laugh, and didn't succeed. "She probably got bored and just went back to town."

"Without a word? Mrs. Weldon is a very old friend of hers. And without taking her suitcase?" Linda asked.

Nelda's lips moved as if they were stiff. She asked, "Didn't she leave a note?"

"No," said Linda, and watched the color return to Nelda's face. She added, "He's driving to town, at once, and I'm going with him."

"You!"

"It seems that I'm the only person who can go," said Linda, "as he doesn't want to be alone. Of course if you wish . . . for if you do," she said, "I'm sure I'd be very happy to —"

"Keep quiet," said Nelda viciously, "he's coming back." She looked at Linda with hostility and hatred. But her face changed as Rix came to the door.

"Rix, I'm so terribly sorry," she cried. "Not that I think for a moment that it's anything serious. Probably Peg just went off to town, French leave, and maybe her friends are the jittery type."

He said, "I know, but it seems queer." He looked at Linda. "I'm ready."

He had no eyes for Nelda. She put her hand on his arm. "But you must have some breakfast, you can't go off like this," she argued.

She was very pretty, her hair loose, her face flushed, her eyes appealing. Rix looked at her, as if with reluctance. He said merely, "Sorry to make all this commotion," stooped, picked up Linda's bag . . . and his own, which was in the corridor.

"Leave them," said Nelda, "Blower will take them to the car. Rix, is there anything I can do, telephoning, anything?"

He shook his head, following Linda down the hall. Nelda persisted, "If there's anything in the world —"

He did not answer.

At the breakfast table he drank a cup of coffee, refused anything else. Blower brought the bags down and Rix's car was brought to the front door. Linda got in, and Nelda stood with her hand on Rix's shoulder. "Promise you'll call me first thing," she said, and he nodded as if he hadn't heard.

The car drove off. Linda, looking back, saw Tony come out of the house to stand beside Nelda, in the morning sunlight.

She said, "Rix, stop in the town and telephone."

They found a drugstore open, and parked the car. She waited with increasing nervousness until Rix appeared. He did not have to speak. His face was drawn with failure. "They haven't heard anything, except that a taxi man took her to a train which left after midnight. Gwen telephoned the apartment but there's no answer," he said.

"Get in and let's go," said Linda.

After a while she said, "Rix, let's stop at the apartment first."

"All right," he said. He added, "It was good of you to come with me . . . I . . . I needed someone."

"That's all right," she said. "Don't look like that. There must be a reasonable explanation."

He said, "Linda, I didn't tell Peg I was going to the Herons' from Easthampton. She must have telephoned Easthampton. She knew the name of the man I had to see. She must have called yesterday — last night — and I suppose they told her I wasn't there. I had left no word where I was going, of course. But when Nelda and I came in from Canoe Place last night, Blower told me there had been a telephone call. For me. No message, just someone inquiring whether I was at Mr. Heron's. He said I was, but had gone out. That was Peg. It must have been."

She said uneasily, "But why — ?"

"You don't understand," Rix told her heavily.

"I think I do. Don't you recall our conversation of the other night," asked Linda, "in the taxi when you were taking me home after dinner? You knew then that Peg was upset about you and Nelda Heron. You asked me if she had been 'complaining.' If you were not at Easthampton where you'd said you'd be, naturally she'd think . . . things. She may have tried your apartment first, and probably did. Then, the Herons'."

He said sullenly, "We had a knockdown fight before she went to the Weldons'. It started because I wouldn't go. It's God's truth that I had this date with old man Martin at Easthampton. He wouldn't come into town, so the firm sent me down. It was an important slice of business if we could get it. Well, I got it. I didn't want to go on up to the Weldons' and start battling all over again with Peg. So I stopped in Southampton."

"Your quarrel was only because you wouldn't go to the Weldons'?"

199

"It began that way," he said.

"And then . . ."

"Oh, Nelda, of course." He twisted around to look at Linda. "All right, so what? So I fell for her. It doesn't mean anything."

"Because it couldn't," said Linda, "because you knew there wasn't a chance; no chance of Peg's divorcing you." She saw his face and asked swiftly, "Was *that* the quarrel, did you ask her to get a divorce?"

"Oh, hell," he said, "I don't know all I said. We were both shouting. I said, 'All right, if that's what you think go ahead and divorce me.' "

"And what did she say?" asked Linda, sick.

"She told me I'd get a divorce over her dead body." The car swerved abruptly and he pulled it back on the road, as Linda gasped. "Over her dead body," he repeated. "My God, Linda, you don't think — ?"

"Of course not," she said stoutly, and felt a cold shiver up her spine as if a feather of ice had been drawn its full length, "of course not. That's — that's just an expression people use. It wasn't meant — Don't look like that!"

"Oh, sure, sure," he said instantly, "she wouldn't do anything so crazy. She isn't the type. She —" He stopped and his mouth worked.

Linda said, "Please, Rix, you're just imagining things."

"Nelda," he said. "Peg couldn't understand about Nelda. You wouldn't, either."

Linda said, after a moment, "Suppose we don't talk? Suppose we just drive. Watch your speedometer, Rix, you don't want to be arrested. Later we'll talk."

It was a nightmare drive. Twice he stopped and telephoned the Weldons and there was no word. He telephoned his apartment as well and listened to the empty sound of the unanswered ringing. When they finally reached there, he managed to ask the doorman and the boy on the elevator, "Has Mrs. Anderson come in?" and each said, "No, Mr. Anderson; I haven't seen her since Friday." The elevator man's eyes slid, too wisely, over Linda, and Rix said, a little too loudly, "Suppose we go on up, I'll leave my bag and then we'll drive on out and meet Peg."

The apartment was terribly empty. The maid had been given the weekend off, she would not return until tonight. It was clean, it was tidy. It preserved its bright and brittle charm, compounded of etched glass and square lines, bright colors and good etchings, plentiful ash trays, deep cushions, the brilliance of copper, chromium, aluminum . . . very "decorated" and decorative.

Rix sat down on the big divan and put his head in his hands. He had gone from room to room, looking. Once he called and his voice was pitiful and uncertain. "Peg," he called, "Peg."

"She hasn't been here," he said superfluously. "Where in God's name is she, Linda?"

Linda sat down beside him. He didn't deserve

pity but he had it in full measure, from her. She was too used to being sorry for Rix and to defending or helping him. You can't escape habit. She said, her hand on his, "Rix, you mustn't think things. She's punishing you perhaps. She's hurt and angry and jealous. She wants you to worry. She'll come back."

He said, "The crazy part of it is, I do love her, Linda. If I hadn't, then you and I —"

"Let's not talk about it," she said, "let's start now for the Weldons' and find out everything we can."

"Wait a minute. I have to talk to someone," he said, much as Peg had said it at the club, "and you're the only person. You see, Linda, I was fond of you, I loved you, I would have been happy with you if Peg hadn't come along. Oh, I don't say I wouldn't have looked at anyone else. There was a girl, when I was in college, whom you never knew about, and someone else, in Boston. But they were just accidental, exciting and fun, they didn't mean anything. Peg was different. I thought, if I couldn't have her, I'd — It was something urgent . . . so . . . But I never dreamed of marrying her. I wanted to, God knows, but I couldn't face you, Linda, my people or yours. And then something happened that —"

She said, "You needn't tell me, Rix, I think I know."

"Peg?" he said slowly. "Did Peg tell you?"

"No, but I guessed," she said, and lied, trying

to save him, to save Peg. "You felt you — had to marry her."

He said, "You'll hate me for saying this, but it doesn't matter, you already despise me. Peg — was pregnant. She told me so. And so we were married. Later she said she'd been mistaken, but I knew she hadn't been. I realized that she had lied to me to — to make me face up to things. I didn't care, really. I didn't tell her I knew. I mean, it was done, I'd walked out on you and the family and that was that. I was relieved in a way. Peg knew me. She knew me better than you ever did. She knew that I'd make the break only if I thought there was a gun at my back. But lately —" He stopped.

Linda felt ill. She said, "All right, Rix, if you want to tell me, go ahead."

"Lately," he said, "there was Nelda. I was crazy about her. I knew that she wouldn't have me on a bet, not if Peg gave me a dozen divorces. I didn't need you to tell me that, the night in the taxi. Okay, I thought, we'll play it her way. She wasn't any more anxious to be found out than I. She wanted to make a good, respectable marriage, one her family would approve of. But of course I said the usual things, would she break with Dennison, would she marry me if Peg released me? I thought I meant them at the time — you always think that — but I didn't, ever. Oh, the Heron name and the money and all that . . . it was plenty attractive but I knew it wasn't for me, not any of it. Besides, I didn't want to be married to her," he said angrily, "a man's a fool to marry a woman like that. What she wants is a lover, not a husband. So she'll have both. She had to have the husband, a husband's a good alibi, and she's very clever. The man who marries her will worship, mostly from afar, he'll be a glorified footman, lady's maid, escort, dancing partner. Nelda Heron," he said bitterly, "would never marry a man whom she really loved — for fear he'd dominate her. She wouldn't want that. She wants to feel condescending, superior, in marriage. With a lover, it would be different; he'd have no hold over her except what she'd give him, no authority."

"Please stop," said Linda desperately, "I don't want to hear any more."

Tony, she thought, Tony, I didn't put up much of a fight for you, did I? I can't let this happen to you. I won't. Not if I have to tell you.

But she couldn't tell him, not now, with Peg gone and Rix half out of his mind.

He said, "Nelda doesn't love me. That isn't love."

Linda said quietly, "I saw you last night from the balcony of my room. You and Nelda. I heard what you said."

"You did?" He seemed scarcely interested. "That's sort of funny, in a way."

"You said you wouldn't give her up — that she was crazy to go through with it. Her marriage, I suppose."

"I know," Rix said. "She'd told me last night

that she wouldn't see me, for a while. She said she thought Peg was beginning to suspect. She didn't know . . . how much, of course. I argued with her, naturally. I didn't mean what I said about her going through with it."

Linda said, "Rix, if you find . . . I mean, *when* you find Peg, will you stop seeing Nelda?"

"I don't want to see her," he said, "not ever."

"I wonder," said Linda. "If Peg walked in this door now, this minute, all the anxiety you feel would turn to anger. I know you, Rix, after all. I've seen you worried and then, when the cause was removed, furious because you had been needlessly upset. If she walked in, could you say truthfully that you were through with Nelda?"

"I told you," he said doggedly. "I love Peg. She's my wife."

"Yet you said she could divorce you."

"I didn't mean it, I swear it," he said despairingly. "It's one of the things you say when you're sore, when you've been quarreling for a long time and are sick of it. I — I told her that I'd known all along that she lied to me, in Benfield, that she'd forced me into marrying her."

"Oh, Rix," said Linda, low.

"I know," he said, "I could kill myself . . . I . . . ." He looked at her and the dark eyes were clear, direct, and wholly honest. "I'm no good. I know it, Linda. Peg knows it. But no one has ever loved me as she does . . . not even you. You haven't the least conception. It's that which would drag me back to her always, no matter what happened. We fight, we call each other names, we destroy each other," he said miserably, "but there it is. I don't care a damn about Nelda Heron. Not really. I won't see her again. I don't say that there won't be other Neldas, along the way. That's the way I'm made. But there isn't a woman who means that much" — he snapped his fingers — "against Peg, no matter what I say, or do."

Linda rose. She said wearily, "Let's telephone the Weldons again — and then go out there and see what they have to say."

A little later they drove out to Westchester, to the pleasant house which Peg's friends had leased. They proved to be a likable young couple, and very much distressed. But there was nothing they could tell Rix that they hadn't already told him.

Gwen Weldon said unhappily, "She telephoned you, Rix, at Easthampton but you weren't there. Then she went to bed, she said she didn't feel well. I came up at eleven or so and later heard her crying. She wouldn't let me in. This morning I went in, early. The door was unlocked, she hadn't slept in the bed. I've told you all this. Johnny telephoned the taxi stands and one man said he'd come out to the house and waited at the foot of the hill as she told him to do and she came along presently and had him take her to the station." She was crying openly. "What could have happened to her?"

"Nothing," said Linda. "Nothing at all. Rix,

tell Mrs. Weldon . . . I mean, that you had quarreled." She looked at Gwen and tried to smile. "I've known Peg quite a while though not as long as you have. You know what she's like. Rix knows . . . she just went back to town, upset over the quarrel."

"Her suitcase?" asked Gwen quietly.

The excuses, the explanations, were too lame to stand on their own feet and so collapsed quietly. Gwen Weldon had known Peg for years, if not intimately. There was definite hostility in her look at Rix.

Johnny Weldon cleared his throat. He was looking and feeling very upset. His weekend was ruined, and the golf he had planned for today. He didn't know Peg. She was his wife's friend. He liked his wife's type, blond, plump, placid. He was slightly afraid of dark girls, who looked as if they might burst into flame at any moment. He had met Peg for the first time in town recently, when Gwen had asked her and Rix to meet them for dinner. He hadn't much liked Rix either. Johnny was a man who distrusts charm in other men. Then Peg had come up for the weekend without her husband. He was sorry for her, sorry for Rix, but why exactly did things of this disturbing, unscheduled nature have to happen to him and Gwen and in their house?

He said, "I phoned the police here, just on a chance there might have been an accident. It doesn't make sense, of course, as the taxi man says definitely that he took her to the station."

Linda rose. "Suppose we go to the taxi stand ourselves," she suggested to Rix. "What did you say the man's name is — Joe Sloskie? We mustn't ruin your entire day, Mr. Weldon."

"That's right," said Rix, "we'll go. I'm sorry, Weldon. Thanks a million for everything."

Gwen was following them to the door. "You'll call me," she begged, "as soon as you find out anything. Promise?"

He promised.

They drove to the office of the taxi stand and it was some little time before Joe appeared. He was a big dark man with an unshaved face. Yeah, he remembered, Mr. Weldon had questioned him, up to the house. Tall, dark dame . . . he corrected himself hastily, tall dark lady, very good looking, said Joe, he'd seen that when she got out at the station in the lights. Yes, she'd 'phoned, he'd taken her call, had had to ask her to repeat the address, she'd just sort of whispered. He waited at the foot of the hill. She said she didn't want to wake her friends. He added that she talked as if she had been crying. She paid him at the station and gave him a good tip. Sure, the south station, going toward New York. He didn't know if she went to New York, of course. That train was a local. It stopped at a lot of places.

But the ticket seller, routed out of his house, remembered. He was on nights. He remembered selling Peg the ticket as she had been the only passenger for New York, on that train.

Rix and Linda drove back to the apartment in silence. They had stopped for coffee and a sandwich, long after the lunch hour, but neither knew they were still hungry. Peg°was not at the apartment. They walked in just as the telephone rang and Rix went scarlet and then white. And Linda said, "I'll answer it."

She braced herself, taking up the instrument, but it was Tony's voice that reached her.

"Linda, what *is* this all about?" he demanded. "Nelda's told me the wildest story . . . something about Peg Anderson . . . and you, dashing off with Anderson."

She said, "It's nothing, Tony, just what Nelda told you. That Peg's been visiting friends and has unaccountably disappeared. I'm certain she'll turn up with an explanation soon. Rix and I have been out to see her friends, and we just got back here."

He said, "I've a good mind to turn you over my knee and wallop you . . . of all the crazy things. I'm coming up there to get you."

"Where are you?" she asked, startled.

"In town. I've called the Anderson apartment half a dozen times. Why are you letting yourself in for all this?" he asked. "Anderson's a grown man, he can handle his own affairs."

She said, "I'm sorry, Tony, you don't understand."

"I understand too damned well," he began grimly.

But Linda replaced the instrument in the cradle. She said, trying to smile, "Just Tony Dennison, wanting to know if we had any news."

Rix spoke as if he hadn't heard her. He said, "Linda, there's nothing we can do now but call the police station . . . and the hospitals."

Chapter 14

There was an atmosphere in this room, a quality in Rix's words, a strangeness in the gathering, sultry dusk that was utterly unreal. Linda stared at Rix. She opened her mouth to speak, swallowed helplessly, and finally found her voice. She cried, "But it can't be, I mean, nothing's happened to her. Surely she's just trying to worry you, or — You'll see," she added, with far more confidence than she felt, "she'll come walking in there at that door, any moment now, and —"

Rix shook his dark head. "There's no use," he said dully. "I tell you, you don't know her." He put his head in his hands and shook. "I can't stand this waiting. We have to do something."

She said slowly, "All right. I'll telephone the — the police."

"Try the hospitals first," said Rix, without moving.

She felt a flare of impatient anger with him, bred from anxiety. Why did he sit there and do nothing? Why must she be the one to act? How did you go about these things? She could have shaken him, in sheer desperation. Let someone else do it! That was Rix. Linda saw in a lightning flash of clairvoyance what her life with him would have been. Oh, happy enough for a time, because

211

she had loved him and her every sense was conditioned to him. But after a while? There would have been other women surely and, always, this burden of responsibility laid upon her, as the stronger of the two, the feeling that, no matter what happened or how much she was hurt, she must excuse and protect him. For the first time she experienced a sharp pity for, and understanding of, Peg. Peg, she thought, is still in love with him, she has always been more in love with him than I. And it's like loving someone who doesn't grow up, except physically.

A woman wanted her man to be fully adult, Linda thought, dialing a number.

She went at it, blind, without any help from Rix, still sitting there, his head in his hands, as if he didn't hear her while she gave the address and the description: age, height, weight. Once she turned to ask, "Do you know what she was wearing, Rix?" but he shook his head.

She hung up after two unrewarding conversations and said briskly, "Rix, pull yourself together. Let's look in her clothes closet, perhaps you can tell what is missing."

He followed her into the bedroom and stood there, his hands at his sides, while she pulled dresses from the closet. This one was too heavy, that one was an afternoon dress. She did not touch the evening dresses in their cellophane bags.

After a while he said dully, "She had a black linen suit, she wore it with an orange blouse, or a green one, she's been wearing it a lot lately; see if it's there."

It wasn't there. Linda asked, turning, "And her hat?"

"She hardly ever wears one . . . especially in summer."

"What an idiot I am!" Linda cried. "Why can't I think straight?" She ran back to the telephone and called Gwen Weldon. It was some time before she reached her, as the wire was busy. When she did, "Have you heard anything?" Gwen asked breathlessly, when Linda made herself known.

"Not yet, Mrs. Weldon. What was Peg wearing, do you remember?"

Gwen remembered. Linda breathed a deep sigh of relief. Black linen suit, lime-green cotton blouse, no hat, beige stockings, black shoes, black handbag. Her other things, a play suit, a bathing suit, a bright cotton frock were, together with her underthings, in the suitcase which Linda and Rix had taken away with them from the Weldons'.

Linda said, after she had hung up, "I'll try the other hospitals."

Before she could dial a number they both heard the clang of the elevator door and the footsteps. Rix said hoarsely, "Someone's coming." He started for the door as the bell rang. He added, and all animation left him, "Peg has a key, she wouldn't ring."

Linda opened the door and Tony stood there, frowning down at her. He came in without invitation and demanded, without preliminaries, "What's all this about?"

"But I told you," began Linda. She found herself irritated. What business was it of his? But under the irritation she was suddenly and profoundly glad that he was there. He was a sane person, he kept his head, his shoulders were broad enough for responsibility.

"Tell me again," he ordered. "Nelda's as vague as a Cape Cod fog. You didn't make much sense either. Begin at the beginning. After all, I'm a lawyer."

Rix roused himself to feeble anger. He said, "It's very good of you, I'm sure, but I don't quite see why —"

Tony turned on him, his gray eyes dark with exasperation. He said, "Look here, Anderson, I don't give a damn what you see or don't see. But if your wife has been taken ill or hurt we have to find her. And Linda's mixed up in it." He regarded Linda without pleasure, and Linda found herself flushing hotly.

"From the very beginning," he repeated firmly.

Rix said sullenly, "You already know she went to visit friends in Westchester and I went to Easthampton and then to the Herons'."

"You can skip that part," said Tony. "Had you quarreled?"

"I don't see what business it is of yours if we did or not."

"It isn't my business," Tony admitted, "but a

simple yes or no might make the picture a little clearer."

"Yes," admitted Rix in some defiance, "we had quarreled. What it was about has no bearing on the matter. If Nelda's said anything to make you think —"

"Just where does Nelda come into this?" inquired Tony evenly.

Linda spoke hurriedly. "What difference does it make why they quarreled? The point is, Peg's gone and we must find her. Do stop glowering at me, Tony!" She told him the rest as briskly as possible while Rix sat in sullen silence.

And Tony asked presently, "Did you try the city hospitals?"

"Not yet. I began at the top and —"

"You aren't very bright," he told her, to her rage. "Peg had no identification on her of course or Anderson would have been notified had she been in an accident and taken to a hospital. If anything's happened, she's probably in a city hospital, and without identification." He looked at Rix. "Call Bellevue and make it snappy."

Rix looked at him, rose and went to the telephone. And Tony took Linda aside, across the room, and standing close to her, spoke low and urgently.

He said, "I didn't think you'd be such a fool."

"What do you mean by that," she asked, "exactly?"

"Getting yourself reinvolved with Anderson," he said. "How much involved and just how far?

215

Because, although I'm no detective, it's pretty clear to me that when Peg Anderson found out he was at Nelda's — with you — and had probably gone there to see you, she —"

"Tony Dennison," gasped Linda, "do you mean to say that you think that Peg and Rix quarreled because of me or — ?"

"What else am I to think?" he demanded. "Good God, Linda, I knew you were in love with him, I knew you weren't over it, no matter what you said, but how could you get mixed up in his life again? It isn't like you," he said angrily. "It destroys every picture I had of you. He's as fine a type of heel as I've ever met but he and this girl are married and even if you're still so blind to his less endearing qualities, you should know better than try to break up the —"

She was so white with anger that he stopped a moment and looked at her in concern. "Linda," he began, more gently, when a sound from Rix reached them. He had turned from the telephone. Now he said, with difficulty, "A young woman answering Peg's description was taken to Bellevue this morning."

He spoke unintelligibly into the telephone, hung up and rose. He staggered a little, as if from a blow, as he moved toward them. He said, "They wouldn't tell me anything . . . much. I've got to go down there. There's a policeman . . . attempted suicide," he said heavily.

Linda gasped. She could not speak. Tony spoke first.

"That tears it. Let's go," he said.

But Rix didn't hear him. He was looking at Linda. He said, "Linda, you'll go with me? *Linda, Peg tried to kill herself.*"

"Linda will stay here," said Tony; "I'll go. If there's any publicity, she isn't to be mixed up in it."

"Don't be an idiot," said Linda coolly. "Of course I'll go, Rix." She gathered her things together and opened the door. She said, "Thanks, Tony, but we don't need you."

"I'm not sure of that," he said grimly, "so I'm going along anyway."

"Oh," said Rix wearily, "what does it matter whether he comes or not?"

"It might matter a good deal," said Tony. "I can pull wires. I can get this hushed up, perhaps. Or to a certain extent. And we'll have her moved when she's well enough. My car's outside. I'll drive."

No one spoke driving downtown. Linda sat with her hands twisted together in her lap. She felt physically ill, cold, dizzy. Peg had tried to commit suicide. Oh, Peg, she thought, poor foolish Peg, he isn't worth it, no man's worth it. She tried not to think of Tony; of what he had accused her. She thought, He wasn't my friend, after all; he didn't know me very well if he could think that. And she couldn't tell him the truth. Not now, with Rix looking as if he had been dragged through a knothole, new lines in his grey face, his hand when it touched her wringing wet, his curly hair wet too, and his forehead.

Well, it didn't make any difference, she thought, and was horrified to find that it did make a difference. To be estranged from Tony was like being pushed suddenly into the cold and dark, expelled from the warm and comfortable dwelling of a friendship so familiar that you did not think much about it until you'd lost it.

Her underlip quivered and she set her teeth firmly upon it. I won't cry, she thought. I won't make an utter fool of myself. But suddenly she could have wished them all out of her life and for good. Tony, who knew her so little, whose friendship could not stand the slightest strain of suspicion — what had Nelda said to him? Rix, with his wavering weaknesses and his helplessness, his perpetual adolescence, who had broken her heart once and seemed like to break it again, after a different fashion; and Peg, loving, unstable Peg, who hadn't enough sense to see that no man was worth — this.

The tears crept from under Linda's tightly closed lids and began to run, warm and salty, down her cheeks.

At Bellevue, she and Tony waited. They did not talk much. Tony smoked, and offered her his case. Linda shook her head. She wasn't crying now, except, bitterly, in her heart. They were not alone in the waiting room. There was little they could say to each other.

Once during their waiting, he spoke. "I'm sorry

if I hurt you, Linda."

"You didn't," she said. "There's no need for apology."

He said, "Of course Nelda was upset —" He broke off.

"Naturally," said Linda, moving stiffened lips, "she would be."

"She likes the Andersons," Tony said lamely.

Well, it was clear enough. Nelda need not have said much. Merely — "If Peg's done anything foolish, if she's run off and left Rix, of course, it was because of Linda Wheaton. She just told me last night —" Was it last night, thought Linda wearily, or a million years ago? — "that she was once engaged to Rix and that he'd jilted her."

Fine. A lovely bit of table turning, thought Linda; nice going, Nelda, and all that sort of thing. She thought absurdly, But Tony's known me longer than he has Nelda. He's known me long and well enough.

He never really liked me, she told herself forlornly, nor really knew me or he wouldn't have thought that. He couldn't have.

Tony said, "He's been there a long time now."

It wasn't long. It simply seemed so. Half an hour multiplied by eternity.

Linda thought, What are they saying to each other?

They were saying very little.

Peg was as white as her pillows, as weak as a newborn kitten, even her lips were white. What she said she whispered, with long pauses and with difficulty. But she was, the doctor said, out of danger.

Nurses, doctors, interns, police. It was a nightmare, a horror.

"You see," she said, "I thought that you and Nelda . . . when you said I could divorce you. I knew for sure about the baby, Rix. I was afraid to tell you. You wouldn't believe me. Because I had told you that before and it wasn't true. And this time it was true. By the time you would have had to believe me it would have been too late because you and Nelda —"

All that took a long time to say. The doctor said that she would not lose the baby. She must be quiet, she must have care. With care and quiet she would be all right.

Rix sat there beside her, and suddenly bent his head to her breast. She was so — helpless. She was like a child who had been lost. A child, carrying his child. For the first time in their relationship he felt an urgent sense of tenderness and protectiveness toward her. Their marriage had been founded on the crazy chemistry of a desire too strong to be denied. They had played at marriage as children play at a game and, like children, had tired. Or he had. They had talked and eaten, laughed and slept together, but they had not been truly married. They had quarreled as children quarreled. He said, "I — if you'll forgive me, Peg, I'll be good to you, I promise, I'll make it all up to you."

"You aren't angry? About the baby?"

"No, darling, no."

She said, "I do need you, Rix."

It was odd, how that made him feel. Perhaps no one had ever needed him before. Not Linda, she had been too strong, that sturdy little girl. Certainly not Nelda, who could manage her own affairs and his too. But Peg . . . who dared try to kill herself for needing him, wanting, and lacking him.

He said, humbly, "I need you too."

I'll try, he thought, walking back to the waiting room. He might not be a signal success as a husband. You don't reform altogether, at his age. But he had never tried before. There'd be upsets and quarrels and all the rest of it. He might not ever be entirely faithful; not his mind, at any rate. But for the first time in his life he faced responsibility and accepted it. And he thought, I do love her better, more, than any woman I have ever known or will ever know. And he knew as well as he knew anything that no woman would ever love him as this one.

In the waiting room, "Let's get out of here," he said abruptly.

Linda stammered, "But Peg?"

"She'll be all right," said Rix, his face haggard, his eyes bloodshot. "Let's get out," he said again, as Linda put her hand on his arm. "I —"

He was conscious of strangers, of curious faces. He had been questioned and he had heard explanations. He was very tired.

"Wait a minute," said Tony. "Here's where I

come in, perhaps." He took Rix's arm and led him to a far corner of the room. Linda followed. No one else was there. He said, "Tell me what happened."

Rix spoke as if it were a story he had learned by rote. He said, "She took the train to New York and went to a small, cheap hotel off Broadway. She told the clerk that her husband would join her in the morning with the luggage. She signed a false name. It seems that she meant to take the suitcase but she thought she heard the Weldons talking in their room as she opened the door. So she left, in panic, without it. She said it might have bumped against the stairs or wall. She had money to pay in advance, so the clerk didn't question her. It was that kind of hotel. She didn't go to sleep. She just lay down on the bed. She was trying to make up her mind. In the morning she made it up. She had this sleeping medicine with her. She had had it ever since she had the flu, shortly after we were married, but had taken very little. Now she took a lot. A chambermaid tried to get into the room in the morning. She went in with her key, hearing nothing, thinking that Peg had gone out. She called the manager and he got an ambulance . . ."

Tony said, "We'll manage somehow. Overdose of sleeping medicine, by accident. I'll see the doctors, Rix, and —"

Rix said, "Thanks." He tried to smile. "Sorry I was so short with you. It would be better because of my family." He swallowed. "I'd be grateful for anything you can do, Dennison."

Linda spoke to Tony. "I'm going back home with Rix and see that he gets something to eat. We'll take a taxi."

"But —"

She said firmly, "We'll take a taxi. I can fix something for him and then he must get to bed."

"Linda," said Tony, "if you walk out of here without me —"

But she had gone, with Rix beside her.

Chapter 15

They took a cab and drove uptown in silence toward Rix's apartment. Once Linda said, "Rix?" and he answered, "If you don't mind, Linda, I'd rather not talk now." His mind was crowded with memorable images: Peg, as he had first seen her, under Linda's familiar, comfortable roof, her integral sultriness so alien in that New England setting, as if you had transplanted a tropical plant, heavy with fragrance, secret with promise, into a tidy New England garden, its borders so neatly marked, its prim posies swept with cool wind, or touched with a gentle sunlight. He was remembering Peg's eyes the night she had told him that they must be married; and again her eyes as he had seen them a little while ago, still drugged, a little glazed with long sleep, but frightened, and appealing; frightened of him, appealing to him.

When the cab stopped he got out, completely forgetting Linda, and found a moment later that she was paying the driver. He said, his hand in his pocket, "I'm sorry, Linda, I was thinking of something else."

"That's all right," she said, "let's go upstairs. I'll get something to eat." Her head felt tight, her hat bound it. She took off her hat and swung it in her hand. This day would never end. And what if it never did, she thought, everything's such a muddle, it doesn't really matter much.

They went on upstairs to the apartment. The shift at door and elevator had changed by now and Linda was faintly relieved, she had expected curious glances, perhaps even questions, or merely, "Mrs. Anderson hasn't returned yet, sir." She shivered thinking how nearly Peg had not returned.

In the living room, closing the door behind him, switching on lights, Rix said abruptly, "I didn't tell you — Dennison was there, and all — but Peg is pregnant. That's —" he swallowed hard — "that's partly why she did it. She thought I wouldn't believe her . . . until too late. She thought I really meant it about the divorce."

Linda said, "Oh Rix," pitifully, thinking of Peg, half out of her mind, wholly out of it, perhaps, with jealousy and grief. Up there, at the Weldons', trying to reach Rix, and then walking down the hill and getting into the cab, taking the train, going to the shoddy little hotel, lying on the bed in that strange room trying to make up her mind.

He said, clearing his throat, "She — she didn't take enough of the stuff to make it necessary for drastic measures. She took enough to make her sick, of course but — Well, anyway, she'll be all right. The baby too. If she has rest and quiet. Linda, she said a funny thing just before I left. She said that when she comes home she wishes my mother could be here."

"Aunt Alice?" Linda's blue eyes were bright. "But that's wonderful." She thought, She's liked her all along, Peg has, wanted to be friends with her. She's known instinctively, about the kindness and strength and love that's in Rix's mother. She's wanted it for her own and hasn't known how to go about claiming it. She said aloud, "Why don't you send for her, when Peg can come home?"

"How can I?" he asked miserably. "She'd have to know then. She'd never forgive me."

Nor Peg, thought Linda, though neither Rix nor Peg would understand that.

She said, "Well, she doesn't have to know, does she? Tony will arrange things somehow. I mean, so there won't be publicity." A thought of the possible headlines flashed before her eyes and she shivered again: Attempted Suicide Identified as Wife of Rix Anderson of Benfield. Oh, New York wasn't Benfield, they'd not play up Rix's absurd name, here.

"Yes," he said, "I know, but that won't help much."

"Don't be silly," she told him; "try to be sensible. All you need tell Aunt Alice is that Peg's started a baby, but nearly lost it and has been in the hospital and needs her when she gets home. That's simple enough, I should think."

The tension in his tired face relaxed a little. He said gratefully, "Thanks, Linda. I suppose . . . Well, it would be swell having her here."

Linda said, "Lie down on the couch and I'll fix some supper. What time does that maid of yours get back?"

"Sometime tonight," he said vaguely. "Peg told her not to bother about dinner or anything."

Linda found eggs, and scrambled them, with milk, the way Rix liked them, put bread in the toaster and coffee in the percolator, and hunted out a jar of jam, some crackers and cheese. When everything was ready she went to call Rix and found him sleeping, his face drained of emotion, innocent in slumber as a tired child's. She looked down on him and shook her head. She felt a troubled tenderness, such as you feel for someone you have known all your life. And pity. But nothing more. She thought, This is where I came in — or rather where I go out. They'll have to work it out between them, he and Peg. I don't want any part of it.

She leaned down and touched his shoulder. Half waking, he said, "Peg?" drowsily and then with an increasing anxiety. Fully awake, he tried to smile. "Sorry," he said, "I was dreaming."

They went into the small kitchen and ate their little meal. Halfway through, Rix set down his coffee cup and asked her, as if for the first time aroused out of preoccupation with himself, "Look, Linda, why was Dennison so sore about your being here?" He frowned. "Why shouldn't you be?" he demanded. "You're our oldest friend."

At her slight involuntary smile he had the grace

227

to color, to shift about awkwardly in his chair.

"Oh, hell," he said, "you know what I mean."

She said calmly, "Tony can be very useful to you in this matter, Rix. I wouldn't antagonize him any further if I were you."

"I won't," he promised eagerly, "I'm sorry about that. I was beside myself. I'm grateful to him of course and always will be. But you — why was he sore at you? I heard a word or two and —"

She said easily, "Oh, nothing, except that I fancy our mutual friend Miss Heron has made him believe that if Peg had done anything foolish it was on my account. Linda," she said wryly, "the home wrecker!"

"Well, of all the damned fool notions," he said blankly, staring.

"How unflattering to you," Linda said, "in a sense." But her attempt at facetiousness was no good, no good at all. She pushed her hair back from her forehead and ate some toast which she did not want. It nearly choked her.

Rix said, "Look here, I'll tell him the truth."

"You'll tell him about yourself and Nelda?" asked Linda. "No, I don't think so. It won't do any good, and it would certainly throw several monkey wrenches into that situation. I don't want to break up another home," she said, and tried to smile.

"But he hasn't any right to think that," Rix told her, "and if you're upset about it —"

She said, "I'm not upset; why should I be? I'm

not interested in the big brother attitude, I can take care of myself, and if that's what he thinks of me, so much the better for his peace of mind and for Nelda. Besides," she added with half a sigh, "I needn't worry about Nelda any more, need I . . . I mean, you and Nelda?"

He gave her a grave, direct glance. "No," he said, "you needn't. Nor Peg. I told her so."

"Okay," said Linda. "Then everything's all right."

A little later she was ready to leave. She said, "You turn in and get some sleep, Rix, you can't see her again tonight."

He had just telephoned the hospital. The report was good.

"I can't thank you enough," he said, "I'll never be able to thank you."

"For what, silly?"

"For standing by."

He put his arm around her as they stood together at the half-opened door and kissed the top of her head, lightly. She experienced no emotion whatever beyond a sudden dreadful fatigue and a longing to be off, out of this apartment and all it stood for in anxiety and waiting, misunderstanding and near tragedy.

His arm tightened. "You're a swell kid," he said.

The elevator door clanged shut. In his preoccupation Rix did not hear, nor Linda in her fatigue. But Tony just stood there and looked at them. He said, "Sorry to interrupt. I've arranged things, Anderson. There won't be any publicity and of course it was an accidental overdose. She'll be able to come home in a few days and your own doctor can —"

Linda didn't hear any more of that. She had released herself from Rix's absent-minded hold and was walking unsteadily away from them, ringing the elevator bell. She leaned against the wall until the car came. She got in and went down and to Rix's car. It was still parked outside. She beckoned the doorman. "You'd better have the car put in the garage," she told him, with a great effort, "or telephone Mr. Anderson and see what he wants done with it. I don't think he will want it again tonight. But he may," she added, wondering if in a case like Peg's there was a danger of relapse. She leaned into the unlocked car and began tugging at her suitcase. She thought in despair, I can't lift it. I can't.

The doorman asked, "Is there something I can do, miss?"

"My suitcase," she began. He didn't know her. He had seen her come in with Rix but how did he know it was her suitcase? Perhaps he believed she was trying to steal something! At the thought, illogical anger seized her and the nervous tears filled her eyes. She said, childishly, "It is my suitcase, I tell you. You can telephone Mr. Anderson and see if it isn't. And I wish you'd take it out of there and call a cab for me."

Tony, coming out of the apartment to stand beside her, said, "Here. I'll take that." He lifted the suitcase out and gave the doorman a coin. "Never mind the cab."

"But I *want* a cab!" wailed Linda.

He took her by the arm and propelled her toward his own car. "Get in," he ordered grimly and she mustered her last ounce of strength to crawl in and sit there like a small and graven image. The doorman watched them drive away and scratched his head dubiously. He was not quite sure whether he had witnessed an attempted — no, an accomplished — burglary, plus abduction, or not. He ambled back to his post. Perhaps he had better ring the Anderson apartment and make sure. He hoped his suspicions were entirely unfounded; otherwise his lack of instant action might be difficult to explain to an irate tenant, manager and, he shuddered, the police.

Tony drove in silence for a block, then halted by a light, he reported unnecessarily, "I'm taking you home."

"Naturally," said Linda, with a sodden sort of sniff.

"Go on and cry," he suggested, without sympathy.

"I'm not crying and if I am is it any of your business?" she inquired with a small, moist show of spirit. "I've been up since all hours — practically all night," she added, remembering the session in Nelda's room, and her own vain attempts to sleep thereafter. Came the dawn, she thought, and what a day!

He said briefly, "Perhaps this will teach you not to be such a little fool." The lights changed, they drove on. He said, "You aren't really in love with him, Linda, you just think you are, from habit."

"Is that so?" she inquired, somewhat aroused. "What makes you think so?"

"You couldn't be," he told her. "You aren't that kind of girl. You — Oh, of course you were hurt, badly, by Rix Anderson. And it was a shock to meet him again. When you told me you were all over it, I knew better. I knew your roots went deeper than that, and that you couldn't get over anything so quickly. But perhaps I was wrong, perhaps you were over it," he suggested, "and this is just a sort of crazy flare-up — and now," he ended, "you've learned your lesson."

She thought wildly, I'll laugh and then I'll cry again? and then I'll be hysterical and first thing you know, I'll land in Bellevue too! Aloud she said:

"Tony, I wish you'd get it through your head. I'm not in love with Rix. He's not in love with me. I came up to town with him to find Peg because he was distraught with anxiety. After all, I am an old friend; not only his friend, but hers. So I did what I could to help and that's all there is to it."

"Does that explain that touching little scene which greeted me when I got out of the elevator?" Tony demanded.

She asked blankly, "But why do you care? I mean, it's so absurd. He put his arm around me, yes. It didn't mean anything to either of us, personally. I was glad he did because I was just about ready to drop, I was so tired. And you're acting like a stuffed shirt, Tony Dennison."

"Thanks," he said, startled. "You change faster than any woman I ever met. I wonder if anyone really knows you."

So now I'm a woman of mystery, she thought wildly, me, Linda Wheaton from Benfield. The Garbo of Benfield, corner of Main and Elm — This is fantastic.

"I don't change," she began stubbornly, "that is, I mean —"

"You don't know what you mean. When I first met you," he said, "I darned near fell in love with you myself. I mean I could have except that Rix was in the picture, solid as a wall, and you were all decked out with no trespassing signs. The thing I liked so well about you was your — well, your happiness, it shone through you like light through crystal. You were gay and gentle and full of fun, and so sure of yourself . . . of the world and your future. It was perfectly wonderful. I was sick to death of girls who were, or pretended to be, cynical and complicated. You were as simple as sunlight and just as welcome. Then next time I saw you, you were different. Here, in New York. The happiness was gone, and you were working at having fun. You were harder and on your guard. It troubled me, but I thought I understood it. It was a sort of camouflage. You'd been hurt, you didn't want to be hurt again. I thought, Well, at least it was a protection. Against the sort of men who didn't know how sweet and —"

"If you say innocent and trusting, I'll murder you!" said Linda.

"I wasn't going to," he said, "but that covers it. Men who didn't know you and took you at your own apparent valuation. Well, I thought, New York's full of wolves and here's Red Ridinghood, fresh out of New England. But that funny little armor you had acquired, even though I hated to see it, I felt would serve you. I watched you and Tom Yorke . . ."

"Tom," she said, "is a reformed wolf, if he ever was one. He has asked me to marry him — Look out!"

Tony dragged the car back into a proper and suitable position, and the taxicab into which he had nearly sideswiped was spared. The wild-eyed driver stopped his cab by the curb and just sat there breathing prayerful imprecations.

"Tom," said Tony, shocked, "isn't a marrying sort of guy!"

"He isn't marrying me," agreed Linda, "if that's what you mean, because I don't want him. And you needn't go running to him with that," she added, "and I'm sorry I told you. I wouldn't have done so — I'm not the put-it-on-the-billboard type — only you make me so darned mad!"

"Well, anyway," said Tony, recovering, "I

thought your new attitude would protect you against Rix Anderson. But it didn't. And I'm disappointed in you. Not that I can't understand your wanting to get back at Peg, I suppose most women would, but to go to such lengths! Of course," he conceded, "if you're really in love with him I suppose there's no telling what you would do." He shook his head. Incalculable girl. He had always liked her so much. He had pitied her, protected her, been her friend. He had never been angry at her before. He was now, clean through. Angry at, disgusted with . . . He said firmly, "I'm ashamed of you, Linda. When I think of that poor girl. . . ."

She said, "We're passing the club. Stop, for heaven's sake. Well, think of her," she added, "all you want. But forget me. Good night."

She made a dignified exit marred by the fact that Tony had to leap out with her bag and carry it up the club steps. He said, "Sorry you're sore, Linda. It was for your own good. And besides," he added in a burst of candor, "I'm so damned disappointed in you. I thought you were different."

"Well, I'm not," she said, breathing fire, "I'm just like anyone else, only more so. A menace," she amplified, "a home wrecker, a — a so-and-so. Spell it any way you like and add a broomstick for camouflage. See if I care!"

"Linda!"

The club door opened, Linda seized her bag and fled. The club door closed, and young Mr.

Dennison returned to his car a puzzled and perturbed young man. In addition to all this uproar, he had quarreled with Nelda. She had been very much annoyed with him when he had torn himself away from her and the joys of a Southampton Sunday, with the avowed intention of following Linda to see that she came to no harm.

He hadn't, now that he thought it over, believed Nelda when she'd told him that if anything came of this escapade of Peg's . . . "If she has run off and left him — and it would be like her to be dramatic — it's Linda's fault. I saw the two of them in the garden last night, Rix and Linda, and when I taxed her with it — honestly, Tony, I can't countenance such goings-on under my roof, now, can I? — she told me brazenly that she had been engaged to Rix, that Peg had taken him away from her but that Rix had realized his mistake . . ."

Because he hadn't believed her he had come to New York. Yet maybe he would have anyway. Now, he didn't know what to believe.

It would take a little time to make his peace with Nelda. She was, and he had known it all along, accustomed to having her own way. Her arrogance was part of her, it suited her, it became her as did her heavy silken hair and her narrow eyes and the atmosphere of luxury and ease which surrounded her. Women were the devil, he thought. They could certainly mess up your life. He was crazy about Nelda, of course, he hadn't thought he'd a chance. He'd rather enjoyed carrying the torch and then out of a clear sky . . . Come to think of it, he hadn't demanded anything of her, hadn't even asked her to marry him. He'd just found her in his arms one evening and she'd said dreamily, "But we can't be married for months yet . . ."

After that, all was as merry as a marriage bell or nearly so. They had had their differences of opinion naturally, but he had told himself that was just a matter of adjustments. And now Linda and that ex-fiancé of hers, and his volcanic wife, not only getting entangled with each other, but disrupting the course of his and Nelda's romance. It was all too much. He thought, I think I'll join the Navy, and found, after a moment, that it was an excellent idea. The law could wait, a war couldn't, we'd get into it, sooner or later, better to be in on the ground floor, or rather, on deck.

Also he had a strange suspicion that his mother wasn't as happy in his engagement as she had been at first. Of course, Nelda didn't pay much attention to her, she didn't realize, perhaps, that older people liked the little attentions. Nelda was too used to being the center of things herself. Not like Linda. Linda was charming with old people . . .

Linda again!

He thought, Well, I suppose I'll see her in the office tomorrow and she won't be speaking to me. He wondered what she was doing now, probably telephoning Rix Anderson, he decided.

Serve her right if Peg recovered and, in her sane mind, divorced Rix and let Linda have him. A proper happy ending, Tony told himself, and wouldn't she rue the day!

He went through a light and it took all his charm, his integral tact, and his legal experience to talk himself out of it. This has been by far the worst day he had ever lived through, he informed himself gloomily.

Linda meantime had gone to her room in the club. Cynthia, entertaining an elderly couple, friends of her parents, in the lounge, saw her trekking past followed by the slower footsteps of the night duty boy who carried a bag. There was something about Linda's back . . . and the way her hair was wild about her face . . . and her hat in her hand.

The elderly couple departed, Cynthia went upstairs and knocked at Linda's door.

"Who is it?" asked Linda, muffled.

"Cynthia." She thought, She's been crying, but hard. "I have a message for you . . . I —"

Linda got up and padded to the door in her bare feet. She said, "Come in. What message?"

Cynthia came in. She said, "Get back to bed. Not that you'll catch cold, it's too hot. I'll sit here. No message," she said firmly, and sat herself down. "It's just that something's wrong. You don't have to tell me, I suppose. You're not the type which confides and heaven knows I can spot 'em a mile off. Only if something's really unpleasant in Denmark and I can help, I'd like you to know I'm at your disposal."

Linda sat up in bed. There was no light in the room except a faint glow from the street. She was a small shadowy shape in a thin nightgown. She said, in a loud, astonished voice, "I haven't a friend in the world. That is, not here. In Benfield, maybe, but this isn't Benfield," and burst into tears.

Cynthia let her cry. After a time she vanished into the bathroom and returned to report practically, "Here's cold water. Nice wet washcloth. And I found some spirits of ammonia. Drink this and don't say anything more if you don't want to. I have some sleeping medicine in my room. If you promise to let me in with it, I'll go get it, give you a pill, tuck you up, and forget this ever happened."

"Sleeping medicine!" repeated Linda, in what amounted to a whispered scream. "If I so much as hear the word, I'll — !"

"Okay, okay," said Cynthia. "But you're wrong about not having any friends. You can't escape friends, you know," she said quietly, "any more than you can escape other important things . . . like birth and love and death, like trouble and taxes and having fun."

"I tried," said Linda drearily.

"Tried what?"

"To escape."

"I see," said Cynthia. A good deal became clear to her in that moment. Linda . . . she liked the little thing so much. Linda was — friendly but she wasn't friends. She was fun to be with but she didn't let you come very close. "Someone has hurt you," said Cynthia, "someone must have hurt you very much."

Linda said, "I don't care now, I mean, you can take just so much, can't you, and no more. It began back in Benfield."

She began to talk and Cynthia listened. It was a simple story, as Linda told it. She didn't try philosophizing or analyzing or go into the psychologies. She merely said that she had known a man all her life and that they had been engaged for a long time and she had been very happy. "I was happy anyway," she said, "I loved everything. My home. My people . . . even my job, but I didn't want a job that would last because I wanted more to be married and have my own place and kids. I didn't care about a career, big or little."

But the engagement had been broken. In a word, Linda had been jilted. Her man had run off with her best friend, so here she was in New York, looking, after all, for a career and not wanting friends, old or new, and heaven knows not wanting a new love.

There's been one friend, however. A man. She liked him, and he was in love with another girl. That's what put their friendship on a solid basis. But then back into the picture came her ex-fiancé and her ex-best friend, now man and wife.

From then on it was a little involved but Cynthia was patient. She sorted out all the relationships after a while. And then she asked a few questions.

She asked, "So you went to Miss Anonymous and asked her to lay off your former and now married boy friend? And she wouldn't? Why did you do that?"

"I didn't want the man who was engaged to her to be hurt," said Linda. "And that was plain or fancy two-timing. The worst kind."

"And after the ex-boy friend and his wife were reconciled tonight," said Cynthia, "why were you still so upset? Wasn't that what you wanted? You don't care for him now, do you?"

"No," said Linda, "and haven't for a long time, longer than I knew."

"And you've forgiven her?" Cynthia pursued relentlessly.

"Of course. I — I'm going to see her as soon as they will let me," said Linda, "I'm so terribly sorry for her, Cynthia."

"Naturally," said Cynthia. "But what I don't understand is, why all the tears now? Those which you can't write off to reaction. Everyone's happy again, and the menace has been removed from the life of your friend, the happy and un-suspecting fiancé of Miss Anonymous." She sighed. "Your passion for discretion makes dis-cussion difficult," she complained mildly.

"His name's Tony," said Linda.

"Tony then. Tony has been restored to his fiancée's arms and will never know that she was faithless," said Cynthia.

241

"Don't joke," said Linda mournfully. "Darn it. Don't you see, Cynthia, he — Tony — thinks I'm the cause of it all. He thinks I plotted to get Rix back." She spoke the names now, unconsciously. "And that it was *because* of me that Peg tried to do what she did. Because of me. Not because of —"

"Miss Anonymous," interrupted Cynthia hastily. "I understand."

Linda said, "I can't believe it. We've been such good friends. If he didn't know me better than that, what was his friendship worth? How do you ever know whether you can trust people or not, Cynthia?"

"You're trusting me," suggested Cynthia, "although I admit you aren't in your right mind. Look. You can, you know. If tomorrow you want it all forgotten, it shall be. I won't mention it again. Not ever."

Linda sighed damply. She said gratefully:

"Please . . . I've wanted to talk to you about everything long before this. But I couldn't. I was afraid. I thought, I won't make friends, I won't be hurt."

"Well," said Cynthia after a while, "I was hurt once, rather badly. No one knows about it, not even Sally. I won't go into it. It's a long story, rather sordid in spots, and dreadfully boring because it happens so often. It's a funny thing that it happens generally to the kind of gals who know all the answers and are pretty sure it couldn't happen to them. You must have wondered why

I took this job. It isn't too exciting. Well, I took it because I once had another job, an exciting one, one I was trained for. Didn't Sally ever tell you I was a laboratory technician? Well, I was. And I met a man while I was working in a laboratory. I fell in love with him and he was married. He had been separated from his wife for a long time. He told me. It was perfectly true. He said he would ask her to divorce him. That wasn't true. He didn't want a divorce, he didn't wish to remarry. He liked playing the field. So," said Cynthia, "I exploded right out of the lab and into the club. It was safer here and quieter. I wouldn't run into him or any of his friends or do the kind of work that reminded me of him. That's what I thought when I took this over. It was some time ago. Now I'm groping out of the fog. And in a little while I'll go back to the work I was meant to do. I have a hunch that women with my training are going to be needed, and badly, before long."

She was silent. And after a moment Linda said, "Thanks, Cynthia."

"Don't thank me," said Cynthia. "One good confession deserves another. I might add here that I had a good friend who saw me through this. You've not met her. She's a nurse and she's gone to England. I don't know what I would have done without her. It's odd, but none of us is very strong. Few can stand on their own feet. We need someone's shoulder to cry on, we need an ear to listen and a hand to clutch, the strongest of us."

"I suppose so," said Linda slowly. "I felt that way about Tony . . . a shoulder, an ear, a hand. He saw me through that awful day when I met Rix and Peg again. I didn't ask him to, he was just there. Now, of course, he won't be there any more. And I can't set him straight," she said, "can I, Cynthia?"

"No," said Cynthia, "you can't. Not unless you wish to destroy his happiness with Miss Anonymous, who sounds to me as if she'd be a lot better off for a slight immersion in boiling oil."

She rose. "I'm going to get that pill. You can take it and sleep with a clear conscience. I'll telephone your office in the morning — we have the number downstairs, I think, on the emergency book — and tell them you won't be in. You haven't slept, you're washed up. You sleep all day and we'll go out to dinner and a movie and you'll turn up Tuesday with a shining morning face."

"But —"

"Hush your mouth," said Cynthia, "and listen to Momma."

When she had gone, the room seemed very empty. She came back presently with the sleeping tablet and a glass of fresh cold water. "Drink this," she said, "Alice in Wonderland."

Linda chuckled, feebly. She obeyed. She said, "I wish you wouldn't go away just yet, Cynthia. I wish you'd sit there and tell me what you think about it all."

"I think you're crazy," said Cynthia gently,

"and I think you're in love with your good friend Tony because if you weren't, why would you —"

Linda sat up. "Oh, for goodness sake," she wailed despairingly, "of course I am. I've been ever since that day when I saw Rix again and — Cynthia," she cried, "I'm such a fool and now it's worse than ever!"

"Of course it is," said Cynthia soothingly, "but there's nothing you can do about it tonight. Lie down, infant, and for heaven's sake go to sleep."

Chapter 16

On Tuesday morning, and with reluctance, Linda returned to the office. She did not feel like the prodigal son; she felt more like the fatted calf, being led to the slaughter. She felt like nothing on earth. She felt on the verge. On the verge of what? Of any number of things: a highly complete nervous breakdown, a volcano with stomach trouble, or manslaughter. It didn't matter. Well, maybe there was something she could do about it, she thought hysterically, in the elevator. She could enter a sanitarium, she could flee the impending eruption, and she could curb, by drastic measures of self-discipline, her primitive desire to strangle Miss Nelda Heron with a strand of her own sleek golden hair. Didn't someone do that to someone in a poem by Mr. Browning? I must, she muttered mentally, ask Professor Phelps.

In short, Miss Wheaton, taking up her briefly interrupted secretarial duties, was in a bad way.

Matters were made, if anything, slightly worse by the solicitous attitude of the office force which, it appeared, had missed her, en masse, on the previous day. Linda received their inquiries in a hair shirt attitude of deep remorse. What a brute she had been, fending off friendly overtures. So darned engrossed with herself and her stupid little ego that she couldn't recognize the sincere give-and-take of ordinary friendliness when she encountered it. She was grateful to find herself alone at last in the Powell office. Mr. Powell, fortunately, was not in town and unopened letters glared reproachfully at her from his massive desk. Work, the panacea, work, the ultimate physician. She seized the letters and a letter opener.

She thought, If Anthony Dennison walks in at that door I'll drop dead! Or jump out the window!

Either method would be an effective way to terminate their acquaintance, she pondered further, with a small, if watery giggle.

The morning passed. He did not come. So what? So, if he didn't, she would drop dead or jump out of the window. Oh, gosh, thought Linda, by nature no Lady of Shalott.

Cynthia had made things very clear. Cynthia had said, sitting beside her, waiting for the sleeping medicine to do its stuff, "You see, it's as I said, you can't escape; you can't escape friends or love or life in general. You can't escape being hurt. Until, or unless, you die. That's part of being alive, Linda, you little dope. You came to New York wrapped up in the cellophane of your pride but it didn't do any good, did it? You wanted to be hard, invulnerable, and ambitious; you wanted to ride roughshod, using everyone you met, men and women, to further your own aims. But you didn't know exactly what your aims were and you hadn't had much experience in riding roughshod or any other way. Also you were yourself. Definitely you can't escape what you are, what you have been for over twenty years, your basic character."

There had probably been more of those pearls of wisdom but Linda herself had been unstrung, the sleeping pill had packed a powerful wallop, and in the middle of Lecture Number One, continuation course in how not to live alone and like it, Linda had fallen asleep.

Came noon, came lunchtime, and Tony had not put in an appearance. Linda went out to lunch with several of the girls in the office. She had joined them in the rest room where they were engaged in keeping their powder dry and their lipstick red. She asked with unusual timidity if anyone was going her way?

During lunch someone remarked that Tony had gone to Westchester to confer with a client who had a bad disposition, arthritis, and a very important suit.

The afternoon went by. Linda telephoned Rix at his office. He reported that he had seen Peg briefly and that she was much better. Linda could see her in the evening if she wished. He'd stop at the club for her. Also he had telephoned his mother. She would come to New York and take over at the apartment and be there ready to receive Peg on her return. Everything, said Rix, was wonderful.

That's what *he* thought!

She was getting ready to leave when her door opened and Tony walked in. His greeting was not gushing. "What happened to you yesterday?" he demanded.

Her knees were weak and she felt as if she had swallowed feathers. She thought in despair and astonishment, So it wasn't a dream or hypnotism, it wasn't Cynthia taking advantage of a weak moment on my part, I am in love with this guy for better or worse and it's going to be worse before it's better. She looked at him and loved every inch of him; a lot of inches. She loved his untidy and mouse-colored hair, and the crease between his brows, his good hands and his square chin, and his gray eyes. And she said, to herself, Well, you certainly stuck your chin out!

She lifted it now in some defiance. She said coolly, "I thought you knew. I was tired. I didn't feel well. Cynthia said you telephoned."

He said, "Twice, but I didn't get much satisfaction. What was the idea of slamming the door in my face the other night?"

"I didn't," said Linda. "Anyway, what did you expect me to do, ask you in for a nightcap?"

"Oh, don't be like that," said Tony, with irritation. "Women!"

Nelda hadn't wanted to make peace with him. He hadn't seen her since Sunday. She sat entrenched behind the sand dunes of Southampton and sniped at him with nasty little steel-jacketed sentences over the telephone wires. She was the sort of girl who likes to dish it out. If you offended, she punished. She had an off-with-his-head complex. Tony had given up telephoning. Let her call him, he decided, and his thoughts dwelt lovingly on the Navy. Every nice girl loves a sailor and that crack about one in every port, but between ports, look what you had? You had a battle-wagon or a flat-top or a tin can or a pig boat and there's nothing aboard those but men, thank God. You've water and lots of it, white water, gray water, blue water. You've a job to do — and probably a spell of mal de mer to over-come — but whatever you have you haven't women. If you break your leg, there's a pharma-cist's mate to take care of you, no angel of mercy in starched white. Good, thought Tony gloomily, let the angels of mercy carry their lamps some-where else. I like it dark.

He looked at Linda. To his astonishment and her horror, her eyes were indubitably bedewed with tears. "Hey," he demanded uneasily, "what's the matter with you?"

"Nothing whatever," said Linda, with all the firmness of jelly. "I'm coming down with a cold."

"At this time of year?"

"People can have colds at any time," she said, "and I wish you'd go away." Her voice rose, the tears spilled over and, as he looked at her agape, she added, with sound and fury, "And stay away. You annoy me. I don't even like you any more. You have a low, suspicious, disgusting mind."

"Well," said Tony, and looked at her as if she were something that had just crawled out of the primordial slime and he was at the business end of a microscope, "if that's the way you feel about me."

The door closed after him, but hard. Also a book, a good expensive well-bound lawbook, crashed against the door the fraction of a second later. And Linda, who should have felt worse, felt better. She picked up the book, restored it to its place — it was never the same again, the case of *Watkins* v. *Mussels* which had established quite a precedent, retained its dog-eared and slightly shell-shocked look for years thereafter — and proceeded to dry her eyes, blow her nose, apply a dash of powder and set out for the club.

That, she thought en route, will fix him. True, she would be forced to encounter him in the office. But as a stranger. And just until she could find another job. Meantime she was through with men. Tom could howl at her door until he had laryngitis but she would be taking a law course, nights. She had no time for male attentions or intentions. When she had a little free time she and Cynthia could go to a movie. Perhaps her father and mother would come down for a week-end. From now on, things would be different. No more emotion. No more anything. Just work and make the best of things. She had a vision of herself, fifty years hence, still making the best of things. Retiring from business, after a testimonial dinner and on an income from investments, to some small white cottage in or near Benfield, beloved by all the neighboring children. A small garden and a cookie jar. The inevitable spinster, who sat up with the ill, advised the young, and tended to her knitting. The vision afflicted her with self-pity, but struck her as funny. Walking up the steps of the club, she thought, Maybe I ought to go see a doctor. I am certainly in need of professional advice. I wonder if there is such a thing as permanent hysteria?

She ascended to her room, flung her jacket, hat and handbag on the bed, and sat down in the chair by the window. She took off her shoes and wiggled her toes. She thought, sanely and glumly, There's no use, my girl, you're in love and there isn't a damned thing you can do about it.

She needn't have been quite so — so final. She could have pretended everything was all right. Then they would have been friends again, after a fashion. At least she would have seen him every day, he would have come in and sat on her desk and dangled his long legs and cracked wise and grinned at her. No, this way was better. A clean break, a sharp severance. The surgical way.

She had never been so unhappy.

What? How could she think that, remembering just last January when Rix had run off with Peg?

But it's different, she thought. Unhappy, yes, and shocked, and wounded. But hadn't her pride hurt most? Where does it hurt? they asked you, the doctors, poking hither and yon. You said, feebly, "Here," or you yelled, "Ouch!" Well, that was the ouch of it. She'd loved Rix, of course she had. It was treason to your own heart to deny a love that once existed, no matter how long ago as heartbeats are counted. But what had hurt most was her pride.

There wasn't a bit of pride in this matter. She was in love with Tony Dennison. He didn't love her. He was in love with Nelda. He was going to marry Nelda. Nelda had not only his heart but his ear. Nothing that Linda could say would make him believe that she wasn't responsible for Peg's presence in a city hospital. Because, listening to Nelda, whom he loved, would quite naturally make him stone-deaf to any other woman's voice. A simple situation.

I'll get over it, she told herself stoutly. I got over Rix. But the odd part of it was she didn't want to get over Tony. She'd had to get over Rix. It had made her ill to think that she had loved him, she had longed to recover quickly, quickly . . . and forget all about it. But loving someone like Tony was different. You could be proud of it. Because he was a real person. He was good, he was decent, he was clever, he was kind. You need never be ashamed of loving someone like that.

Of course, he was also an idiot. But that was Nelda's fault. All men are idiots when they are in love. And women too. With which profound deduction she prepared to eat her dinner and wait for Rix to call for her.

She had a little time alone with Peg at the

hospital. She was embarrassed, looking at Peg's drawn face against the pillows, and the big gray eyes, deeply shadowed. She was embarrassed because Peg had no defenses, Peg was vulnerable and human, and soft, and because Peg spoke to her from her heart.

"I've been such a fool," said Peg, in her husky voice, "and you've been wonderful, Linda. Rix told me."

"That's all right," said Linda, with extreme awkwardness.

"He told you," asked Peg, "that everything's — fine? I mean, between us? I was such a fool," she said again, "to go off like that. Off the beam, really. I believed him, you see. About Nelda and everything. And I was frightened because I knew about the baby. I thought he wouldn't believe that. I didn't care what happened to me, to — to us." She stopped and Linda patted her hand. And Peg went on, "Look, Linda, it's just that I love him. I haven't any illusions about him but I can't get along without him. It's weak of me, it's part perhaps of — of my punishment, that things are this way. They'll always be this way. But next time I'll be different, I'll be patient, and wait. He'll always come back, you know; somehow I'm sure of it. Did he tell you his mother's coming down?"

"Yes. I'm so glad, Peg."

"So am I. Perhaps," Peg said wistfully, "she'll grow to like me. I always liked her a lot. But she was so crazy about you — and then I thought she'd never like me because of what I did and it made me say and do the wrong thing, I felt so guilty toward her . . . making trouble for her, because of Rix . . . but now maybe she'll forgive me, after a while."

"Of course, she will," said Linda, "I'm sure she already has . . . and she's going to love being a grandmother."

"It's more than you can say for most women nowadays," said Peg, with the ghost of a chuckle.

It was time for Linda to go. She went out to the waiting room and sent Rix in to see his wife. Waiting for him, there with all the anxious strange people — you could feel their emotions, you could almost touch them they were so tangible, fear, impatience, patience, hope — she thought, He hasn't told her anything, merely that I left Southampton with him and stayed with him until he found her. Well, that's just as well. What good would it have done to say anything else?

But Peg, being a woman, didn't have to be told in so many words. She looked at Rix as he sat beside her and asked, "What's wrong with Linda?"

"Nothing," he answered, astonished, "that is, nothing I know about."

"There is too," said Peg, "she's different. Something's happened. Was — has it anything to do with us, Rix?"

Rix said, "Of course not. And I don't know what you're talking about. Oh" — his brow cleared and he said comfortably — "Tony Dennison maybe. He was sore at her. For leaving the Herons' Sunday with me. I told you he came to the apartment." He stopped and shrugged. "Of course, he thought that Linda was the cause — of all this."

"You're a goop," said Peg, a little color in her cheeks, "it's clear enough to me. She's in love with him, isn't she? I've thought so for some time."

"Why?" demanded Rix, astonished.

"Well, she isn't with you," said Peg calmly. "I thought so at first but when I became convinced that you were no longer headman, naturally I wondered about Tony. Who gave him that idea," she demanded, "about Linda, I mean?"

"Nelda," said Rix, and flushed.

"Good Lord," said Peg, "men!" She lay back against the pillows. "That settles it," she said. "Linda's crazy about him or she'd tell him the truth."

"I don't get it," said Rix.

"You sound like Gracie Allen," said his wife. "Don't you see how her mind works? If she wasn't in love with him she'd march herself up to him and — Rix, don't look so miserable, it's all over and done with, dear — and you know what she'd say. But being Linda she can't say it. Because he's engaged to Nelda, because he's in love with her — or so Linda thinks. I never thought so."

Rix looked at her, his jaw slack.

"You never thought so?" he repeated feebly.

"Certainly not," said Peg. "Nelda's a glittery sort of bait. Almost any poor fish would rise to it. She can turn the charm on and off. She turned it on like anything because it was — well, expedient. And he'd been going around thinking she'd never look at him — she used to treat him badly, you know that, we all saw it — but I don't think he minded too much. It was like falling in love with someone across the footlights. You really don't expect anything. It isn't the kind of love you expect to live with . . . and see evenings in curlpapers or across the kitchen table," Peg explained. "Then when she suddenly unbent — oh, there's no use trying to explain it to you," she said crossly, "you're a man too. Rix," asked Peg, "do you really love me?"

His reply was as satisfactory as possible under the circumstances.

"Maybe," said Peg, twinkling faintly, "we can do something about Linda."

Rix looked alarmed. He asked, "What? I mean, you wouldn't . . . that is . . ."

"Leave it to me," said his wife serenely, "I'll dream up something. We owe it to her," she added, and looked at him soberly. "We owe her — a lot, Rix."

"I know," he said, with humility.

He added, after what seemed a long time, "If you think it best, Peg, I'll see Dennison and make a clean breast of it."

"That would be just wonderful," Peg told him; "you'd get a sock in the jaw from Tony." She shook her head. "It's one of those honor rooted in dishonor cases, Rix. We can't solve it that way, you know."

He looked relieved. Well, that was Rix. You couldn't expect him not to look relieved, could you?

Linda's law class opened. She went to school nights, with books, notebooks, and a brief case. Mr. Powell congratulated her upon her undertaking. "If," he suggested, "you can manage? There's an old warning about burning your candle at both ends, Linda."

Linda said, "I'll manage," and grinned at him. "Both ends against the middle?" she asked. "But don't worry, Mr. Powell. If I can't carry the work," she said, "I'll drop it."

He thought she meant the law class; she didn't. She still had her legacy, and she had saved some money. Mr. Powell paid a generous salary. Drop Mr. Powell, go on with the law, and someday go back to Benfield and into her father's office. That made sense. Besides, if she left the office she'd never see Tony. Her heart parachuted into her boots. Silly, she told it, and hauled it up again.

She was seeing him every day, or almost every day. "Hello," he said, and she said hello and that was all there was to it. Nice aloof courtesy. Friendship, love, indifference, hate. Well, Tony had hurdled the love angle and reached the indifference stage. There wasn't anything she could do about it.

Peg went home, Aunt Alice came down, Linda went to see her. Funny how her relationship with Peg and Rix shook down to normal as if Aunt Alice held it up like a thermometer. Linda knew how she stood with them, and they with her. And it was pleasant to have a place to which she could go and where, at last, she felt both at ease and welcome.

She had a farewell dinner with Tom Yorke, who was leaving the office. A job in Washington. It might turn out to be a big one. Linda had refused his invitations all autumn but now she relented and dined with him one blowy Sunday night in November. He said, looking at her across the table, "I was serious about you, you know."

"Past tense, I hope," she murmured.

"No. But I know when I'm licked." He smiled at her, engagingly. "If you change your mind you know where you can find me."

"I shan't," she said, "but you're a swell person, Tom, and I wish you all the luck in the world."

"This job," he said, "it may mean something. I don't know. I've been thinking of the Army. But I'd probably get stuck in the Judge Advocate's office. This is better, I think, as long as I can't get combat. It will mean doing a job. Not that I don't regret the uniform. I think I'd look very pretty in uniform," he added, grinning.

"Beautiful," she agreed. She frowned a little. "Combat? You really think we'll get in, soon?"

"Of course. And so do you. So does everyone. I was talking to Tony the other day. I suppose you know he wants to go into the Navy, if they'll take him, not as a legal light but as a plain common, or garden, gob."

"No," she answered, and it was hard to admit it, "I didn't know."

"You two been fighting?" he asked. "I thought so. Well, better kiss and make up. Tony's a fool," he added; "he doesn't know which side his bread is buttered on."

Linda thought, Better not ask what he means by that. Her throat felt tight.

"You're not too bright either," said Tom; "someday you'll find it out. I won't help you. I'm not that magnanimous. Did I forget to tell you you're looking very pretty tonight?"

"You never forget," said Linda. She thought, I'll miss Tom. She didn't want him, but she would miss him. He was a tonic spirit. He was good for the weakened ego. He was a shot in the arm, if not an arrow in the heart.

Tom grinned at her cheerfully. "I wish you'd go see my family when I'm away. They like you. You're the only girl I ever loved of whom they approve."

She said sincerely, "I shall, Tom — some Sunday perhaps. I'm pretty busy these days."

"I know. You'll make an attractive Portia," he told her, "although woman's place is definitely in the home and not before the bar. Any bar." He lifted an eyebrow and added mildly, "Do you see what I see? Can it be ectoplasm?"

Linda followed the direction of his regard. The

room in which they were dining was small, crowded, expensive and exclusive. It was known among its habitués as the Needle Eye. The richer you were, the harder to get in. You engaged your table several weeks in advance, and if you were really known the measured insults of captains and headwaiters were almost affectionate in tone. This sort of treatment is doted upon by New Yorkers. They love to be made uncomfortable.

The bar was not large, it had high red stools and the bartender was known as a character. Order an old-fashioned and he suggested that you'd already had one too many. How was your liver? His name was Joe. Everyone was crazy about him.

There were many people at the bar, too many. No one was being served — Joe was the type you had to wheedle. As there was no room, two more people had joined the fraternity of camels. One was Nelda and the other was Tony.

"Reunion," said Tom resignedly, "in Gehenna." He beckoned a waiter and said with the proper amount of irritation, "I want a telephone."

One was brought and plugged in. "What on earth?" Linda began. She thought, I hope they don't see us. She thought, Is he really joining the Navy? She thought, Maybe I'd better marry Tom, after all, I'll make a heck of a lawyer. She thought, Nelda's looking wonderful. I hate her. I hope Joe gives her arsenic.

Tom spoke into the receiver. He said, "I don't

know if this is the house switchboard or an outside wire."

It was the house switchboard, a voice informed him coolly. Tom replied, "Oh, sure. Stupid of me, sweetheart. Otherwise you get stung with calls to Hollywood. I want the bar. Bar." He spelled it. "That's it, sister — Joe, at the bar. There is absolutely no other way of attracting his attention."

There was an interval. Tom spoke again. As he spoke, Linda opened a compact and peered in the mirror. She could see one anxious blue eye. It seemed to be in its usual position.

"Joe? Yep. Tom Yorke. Yes, of course. At a table in your unprintable joint. If you don't believe me, look over." Linda, laughing in spite of herself, saw Joe turn from the telephone and look, incredulously. "I want to speak to a friend. He's crossing the bar. More or less. Page him, will you? A Mr. Anthony Dennison. If you get through to him drop a highball glass as a signal. No, I'm not stinking," said Tom severely. "Tell him he's wanted at the worst table a generous man ever slipped Frederick twenty bucks for . . . yes, in the corner, and so close to the pantry door that the management includes a free haircut with every entrée."

"He hung up," said Tom mildly and did likewise.

They could hear Joe's heavy accents. "Mr. Dennison," said Joe, "hey, Mr. Dennison."

Fascinated, Linda watched. She saw Tony's

tall head, she saw Joe pushing people out of the way with large sweeps of hamlike hands. She saw Tony turn to survey the room, she saw Nelda turn.

Nelda wore black. She had been poured into it and set aside to cool. She wore a sable coat. She wore her own golden hair, and a new mouth painted over the one God had given her.

"Tom!" cried Nelda in the usual table-hopping scream. "Linda!"

Carrying their glasses they descended upon the corner table. "Two more chairs," said Tom to the waiter. "Of course, there's room." He looked at Nelda. "Why should you want to be alone with him," he asked, jerking a thumb at Tony, "now that he's hooked? Did you know I was going to Washington? Yes, it's been discovered that I'm one of the few men extant who can recite the alphabet backwards. They need such mental giants there."

He kept her talking. He suggested, "Why not have dinner with us now that we've almost finished. Nelda, you look like a squirt of Vichy in a blackout."

Tony looked at Linda. He said brilliantly, "You're looking very well."

"I'm fine." Her heart hammered in her throat. She thought distractedly, I wish I hadn't eaten so much. "Tom tells me you're thinking of joining the Navy."

Tony muttered something about a commission in the Reserve. And Nelda, who had more than

263

her share of ears, leaned across the narrow space and smiled at Linda. She said, "Of course, he isn't. That's just conversation. We aren't going to war. People panic too easily." She shrugged. Then she added sweetly, "How is poor dear Peg?"

"She's all right," said Linda, and felt the blood leave her heart.

"Dreadful, wasn't it? I never could understand this overdose business," Nelda said, "as if you didn't know how much of anything you take!"

Tony spoke, in a hurry. He said, "Let's grab our table, Nelda, or Frederick will give it to someone less attractive."

"So nice to have seen you two," said Nelda, smiling, and rose.

When they had gone Tom asked, "What did that mean, if anything?"

"What?" asked Linda abstractedly.

"About Peg . . . Peg Anderson, I take it."

"Nothing. That is, she took an overdose of sleeping medicine," said Linda evenly, "by mistake."

Tom lifted an eyebrow. He said, "I hadn't heard."

"Of course, you heard," said Linda angrily, "everyone has. You were in Southampton that day, you must have —"

He said, "So that's it. My dear child, I not only heard but I saw a thing or two. Are you letting Nelda get away with this?"

"I don't know what you mean," said Linda. Her mouth shook.

"Okay. Have it your way. You haven't ordered your sweet," he told her. "How about Cherries Jubilee? They do them very well here."

"I don't want anything." She thought, It isn't fair. I'm always seeing people when I don't expect to and going to pieces about it. She looked at Tom. "I'd like to go home," she said. "It's so terribly warm in here."

"All right." He beckoned the waiter. The check came and the sum involved would have fed a regiment. Tom paid, unflinching. He said, "Let's go, and I won't say anything more, Linda, but it isn't as if they were in love with each other. They aren't. Nelda's not capable of being and Tony's on the startled and chivalrous side. I don't know why I'm telling you this. Do you suppose my mother was frightened by Sydney Carton before I was born? Nobility's catching up with me."

Linda was on her feet, the waiter was helping her with her coat. She thought, If I can only get home before I start crying again.

Chapter 17

Several things came of that evening. For instance, the encounter between Tom and Cynthia. He went into the club with Linda and there was Cynthia. They had not met before. They said, "Hello" and "How nice," and Tom thought, That's one of the most attractive girls I've seen yet; she isn't pretty but there's something . . . And Cynthia thought, Linda has all the luck. Months later a government laboratory job took her to Washington, and their second encounter was in Rock Creek Park. But that's another story.

What came, more immediately, was the quarrel between Tony and Nelda. It got under way when they had reached their table. "What was the big idea of that crack about Peg Anderson?" he asked.

"Crack?" repeated Nelda, one satin eyebrow raised. "Really, darling!"

"You know what I mean."

"I didn't say anything except to ask how Peg is. If Linda looked guilty, it isn't my fault."

Rix, she thought. She hadn't seen him since that horrible Sunday. She had telephoned him and he had said, brutally, that she wouldn't be seeing him again if he could help it. So the entire pattern fell to pieces around her. Not that she cared. There were other men.

But she missed him. The excitement, the planning, the scarlet thread of intrigue woven through her days. She despised him now, of course. And Tony bored her. He had been so different since that day. Not at all as she wished him to be, easily maneuverable.

"I was crazy," said Tony doggedly, "to believe anything you said, for a minute." He looked at her and shook his head. How did you tell the woman you were to marry that she was a liar, that you'd caught her out in a dozen trivial falsehoods? If she had lied about Linda, it wasn't trivial.

She had lied, no matter what the circumstantial evidence . . . Linda's past love for Rix Anderson, her presence in his apartment that Sunday, his arm about her at the door.

Why should I care so much? he asked himself, knew the answer immediately and was so disturbed that he set down his highball glass with special care lest it shatter in his hand.

Nelda complained, "You've been so *dull* lately, Tony."

By the time they went on to the Southwocks' party — one of the famous, slightly drunken Southwock evenings, half of Broadway and Tin Pan Alley, most of Park and Fifth, and certainly all of Writers' Row — they were not on speaking terms.

Early Monday morning, Tony left Nelda at her apartment. He said, "I'm sorry, Nelda."

How do you tell a woman that you're sorry but only because it's been such a hideous evening and you hate quarrels and recriminations? How do you tell her that you sat across a room full of smoke and noise, looked at her dispassionately and decided that she'd had too much to drink, that she looked haggard and hard, and her voice was pitched too high? How did you tell her you didn't love her and that you never had? That you'd been crazy about her once, which isn't the same thing, and had expected nothing, and when it came to that, had wanted nothing except to be near her now and then and look at her? How did you tell her that you'd never believed she'd marry you and hadn't really wanted her to? How did you tell her that you were in love with someone else and had been ever since a blue day, shot with gold, over a year ago, when you walked into a law office and found her there, to learn shortly afterward that she belonged to someone else? So, you didn't think you'd been in love even for ten minutes, because things didn't happen like that.

You didn't tell Nelda anything. You said good night, and went away.

A night or so later Alice Anderson had dinner with Linda at the club. She reported that Rix and Peg were fine. And there was wonderful news . . . Rix was going back to Benfield.

"Aunt Alice!"

Mrs. Anderson nodded. "Back to his father and the bank," she said.

"But Peg?"

"She urged it. She's a sensible girl, really. If we get into this war —" she shook her white head — "Rix is sure we will. He'll go, of course." There was a little catch in her voice. "Peg says if he does she would want to be — home. With us. And Benfield will be better for the baby."

"It will be better for all of you," said Linda. "But won't they miss New York?"

"Rix says not. And Peg says she's had enough of it. Oh, no doubt, at first they had all that goes with it," said Mrs. Anderson, "but since her illness, nearly losing the baby . . . Having a baby will make a difference, Linda. A child should be brought up in a small town," she said, "with all a small town has to offer."

"Yes, I know," said Linda. She swallowed. "When are they going back?"

"Before Christmas. We're going to make the second floor into an apartment for them, with their own living quarters, kitchen, everything. The house is so big. In this way they'll be with us but can be by themselves, as they should. We're delighted about it. Of course, the apartment won't be ready for some time but it will be, long before the baby's born."

She talked about the apartment plans but Linda didn't hear. She was thinking, They're so lucky.

Mrs. Anderson spoke to Peg the next day. "I'm

worried about Linda," she said, "she isn't at all like herself. She looks downright peaked. Pinched and thin, and half the time she doesn't know what you are saying, she's so abstracted. I wasn't with her long. She had to go to law class. I think she's overdoing and I'm going to write her mother and tell her so."

"No," said Peg, "don't." She smiled at her mother-in-law. "Linda would hate that. Don't worry, I'm sure she'll be all right. Perhaps the class is too hard for her to carry but she'll drop it once she finds it out. Better let her work this out herself, mother."

"Perhaps," said Alice doubtfully, "but it takes the heart out of me to see her . . ." She thought, Last winter I was terribly worried about her but I understood what was wrong then. I don't, now.

Peg looked at Alice. "Can you keep a secret?" she asked.

"Naturally," said Mrs. Anderson, with dignity.

Peg smiled. She said, "Linda's in love. Don't look so startled, dear. It's all very suitable. I can't tell you any more than that except that it just isn't going very well at the moment. But it will. You'll see."

I'll see, she thought.

It was the hardest thing she'd ever had to do, but she had told Rix that they owed it to her. And she'd do it. She had put it off, from sheer cowardice. Now she wouldn't put it off any longer.

No one could have been more astonished than Nelda to find Peg on her doorstep, so to speak. It was early in the morning and Nelda had just finished breakfast. She was writing letters in a little room off the library when Peg was announced.

Blower, the imperturbable butler, thought it odd to see Nelda undecided. She wasn't at home. Yes, wait, she was at home.

Peg came in, dark, lovely, smiling faintly. She said, when Blower had closed the door, "I'm sorry to barge in like this. But I came for two reasons. One is to say good-bye."

"Good-bye?" Nelda repeated, startled.

She was wearing ice-blue pajamas, the jacket edged with mink. She looked as remote as a fairy-tale princess. I don't blame you, Rix, thought Peg. That is, not much. Yes, I do. I always shall but you'll never know it.

Peg hadn't taken Nelda's hand. She sat down, at Nelda's gesture. "I won't take long," she said. "Rix and I are going back to Benfield, to live with his parents. I'm having a baby," she went on evenly and was pleased to see Nelda's altered expression. "And we think we'll be better off, out of town. Especially if there's a war, because Rix will go, if there is — he won't wait for his number to be called. And another thing, I never acknowledged the flowers you sent me in the hospital." She added, "They gave great pleasure to the ward to which I sent them."

Nelda said, "I didn't expect you to acknowledge them."

"No? And I wanted to tell you that I'm delighted about your broken engagement," said Peg, and smiled at Nelda cheerfully.

"My broken — What do you mean?" Nelda demanded. "Have you lost your mind? My engagement hasn't been broken."

"It will be soon, won't it?" asked Peg pleasantly. "The little notice in the papers that you're back in circulation will interest a lot of people."

"Why don't you come to the point?" asked Nelda stonily.

"Pen point," agreed Peg. "You shouldn't write letters. Rix shouldn't leave them around. But he did. One, that is. Before I was — ill."

She held her breath. It wasn't quite a lie. There had been letters. Rix had brought one home from the office one day by mistake. Just the envelope, however. Peg knew the writing. She hadn't seen the letter. Not that I wouldn't have read it, she thought, if I'd had the chance. I'm not above that, nor anything, I suppose.

Nelda was very pale. She asked, "What do you intend to do about it?"

"Nothing," said Peg. "You'll do it."

"You're trying to tell me that you'll go to Tony . . ." began Nelda.

"I'm not telling you a thing," said Peg, and rose. "Good-bye," she said, "it's been unpleasant knowing you."

"Wait," said Nelda. She asked slowly, "Just —

272

why? You're going back to wherever it is, you and Rix. Why all this, now?"

"Oh," said Peg, "no special reason. Except that Tony's a nice person. I think he deserves a break. You know what kind."

And was gone, her heart and knees unsteady. But she thought, reaching the cold outer air, hailing a taxi, She'll do it, because she's afraid. She doesn't know what I'll do. That's what frightens her. She could fight facts but not this. She'll think . . . anything. She won't dare go to Rix. It doesn't matter if she does.

Riding home in the taxi she thought, Good luck, Linda, maybe I've made it up to you. I hope so.

Tony, at the office a day or so later, remembered he had something to discuss with one of his senior partners. He opened the door to an anteroom and looked in. There was a girl sitting there. Her name was Linda and she was twenty-three. Her hair was the tawny chestnut of October hills and her eyes were blue as the autumn heavens. Her hands on the typewriter keys were small and strong. She looked like a girl he had met in New England over a year ago, but she did not whistle as she worked, her face was thin and her lipstick a defiance. There were shadows under her eyes. The girl he remembered had looked happy enough to fly.

She didn't hear him come in, and she didn't hear him go. She was very busy and the typewriter chattered like a magpie.

Tony shut the door softly. He could wait to see Powell. He wanted to think.

This is your girl. You love her, you want her. Nelda was never your girl. You are going to tell Nelda that, tonight. You are going to be crass and honest. You are going to say, "I don't love you, Nelda, I love someone else." Nelda won't care, except with the surface of her mind. You'll ask, "Will you release me from our engagement?" She won't care, because she doesn't love you, she never has.

Linda doesn't love you either, but you can spend the rest of your life trying to make her.

Tony returned to the Powell office. He opened the door wide and said, "Hi, Linda," and she jumped, and the magpie fell silent. He shut the door and stood over her at the desk.

"I came to ask you to forgive me," he said quietly.

"For — for what?" she stammered, taken wholly aback.

"For saying all I did. For believing it, even for an instant. I didn't, really. I was jealous. Of Rix. Linda, I wouldn't have believed it if I'd seen it with my own eyes. Don't sit there looking at me as if you were going to pass out," he ordered crossly, tenderly. "I'm not going to tell you I love you and always have, because through some insanity which I'll try to explain later I'm still engaged to another girl. I won't be, this time tomorrow. And don't say anything, I know you don't even like me now. But if I try, if I — Stop looking like that," he said, and his voice rose, "or I'll forget I'm still engaged."

The door banged behind him and Mr. Powell erupted from the inner office. "Who on earth . . ." he began, "all that noise and confusion, who . . ."

Linda sat perfectly still.

"Linda, who was that?" said Mr. Powell.

She said in a loud amazed voice, "It was Tony Dennison."

"What did he want?"

"He didn't say," Linda answered, "but I think I know." Under her employer's startled eyes she bloomed with color, her eyes shone and she looked happy enough to fly.

"Is he coming back?" demanded the bewildered Powell.

"Of course," said Linda, "tomorrow."

"Well, I'll be damned," said Mr. Powell, and retreated to his office. Someone was crazy. Could it be himself?

Linda's fingers flew. She was writing to a Supreme Court Justice. "Darling," she wrote, "I'm so happy, darling, darling . . ."

She took it out of the typewriter and tore it up. Just as well. The Justice was young and healthy but a stroke wouldn't improve him, and he was a busy man, no time for strokes.

She thought, This time tomorrow —

At eight-thirty that evening Mr. Dennison presented himself at the home of his fiancée. He had telephoned to ask formally if she would receive him. No, he wasn't going out of town as he had expected. He had postponed his trip.

They sat together in the drawing room. Fortunately for Mr. Dennison, the elder Herons were dining out. None of their paternal, Tony dears and Tony my boys. They would be a hurdle. But as they denied their child nothing, surely they would not deny her a broken engagement?

"Well," asked Nelda, "what's on your mind, my sweet?"

She spoke lightly. She thought, Get it over with. She thought, I've found I made a mistake. I'm very fond of you, Tony, but —

Tony cleared his throat. All the phrases he had practiced, mentally, fled. He said, with great directness, "We don't love each other, Nelda. Shall we call it off?"

Nelda looked at him in stunned silence. She hadn't had a chance. She had been jilted!

She said, after a minute, in a tight voice, "That's odd, as I was trying to find the courage to tell you that I felt we were making a mistake."

He'd never believe it. Never. He'd always think she'd said it to save face. He mustn't get away with that.

She saw his instant relief, she thought she saw the slightly skeptical quality of that relief, and she added quickly, "I never loved you, you know."

But he was armored, she couldn't hurt him.

He nodded. He said, "I've known it for some time, Nelda."

Don't let him get away with it. Make it stick. Say hard, cruel, ego-wounding things.

Her smile was painted on. She said, "There was another man."

She saw his shock, she heard him ask incredulously, "Then — why?"

"Oh," she said carelessly, "we couldn't marry. It was — rebound, I suppose."

Let him build up that picture. He would never see the true painting underneath it.

Tony rose. "Thanks for telling me, Nelda. You'll tell your parents and make all the gestures?"

She rose too. "Well, fun while it lasted. Shall we kiss and be friends?"

"No," said Tony, "I don't think so."

Leaving the apartment, he thought, So it was Nelda. Nelda and Rix.

A hundred memories came to mind, unrelated things he had seen and heard. Nelda and Rix. And Peg had known. Linda had known. Linda could have told him. She wouldn't. She would never tell him.

He called himself several names. He called Nelda a name or two. But then he found himself laughing, crazily, walking down the wide street in a sudden flurry of snow. What did it matter, what did anything matter? He was free.

Linda was in bed when Cynthia came to knock at the door and to tell her she had a telephone call. "He says that if you're asleep I'm to wake you," said Cynthia. "He says, 'Tell her it's Tony.' "

She watched Linda fly past, mules clattering, her robe huddled around her, down the back stairs to the booth which was out of sight of club visitors.

"Tony?"

He said, "It's all right. I called you to say just that. Everything's fine. I love you, Linda, and I'll see you tomorrow. Good night, darling."

In the morning he walked into the anteroom of Powell's office. There she was, sitting at a typewriter, tawny hair and blue eyes. She looked happy enough to fly. She whistled while she worked. She shone as if you had picked her off a Christmas tree.

He asked, "Could you learn to like me — again?"

Somehow she was in his arms, somehow he was kissing her and everything was perfectly wonderful. And after an interval she said, "I should make you wait," and after another interval he said, "We haven't time, we're going to Benfield to be married. Mother will tag along. I told her this morning I was switching daughters-in-law on her and she's enchanted. She wants to see you."

Linda drew back. She cried, "You're that sure of me."

"Yes, of course," said Tony contentedly, "for if you'd been just my good little friend, Linda, you would have told me about Rix Anderson and Nelda. But you didn't. Why? Because you were in love with me," deduced Tony modestly, "and you were afraid I'd think —"

She interrupted, "Tony, she — she didn't *tell* you!"

"Trapped," said Tony happily. "No. I was pretty damned dumb, I suppose. By the way, it appears that Nelda was going to break our engagement anyway. So —"

"I don't believe it," said Linda stoutly.

"That's handsome of you. Linda, we'll wire your family today, we'll be in Benfield by — how about Sunday? And married as soon thereafter as possible."

"But —"

"No buts. I'll take a vacation, I have it coming. We'll go south till the first of the year."

Linda's calendar was on the desk. She said, "But this is only the third."

Wednesday, December third, nineteen hundred and forty-one.

He said, "And then we'll settle down until the Navy wants me. You'll make a very attractive fleet follower, darling."

"My law class," she began helplessly, "my —"

"Husbands," he said grandly, "are more important. You know all the law you need know. What you don't know I can teach you. Darling —"

"But there's so much to — say."

"We have the rest of our lives," he told her,

"in which to discuss it. Kiss me, and make it snappy. Not too snappy," he amended hastily, "but I have to be in court today and I won't see you until tonight and that's years. Meantime you send the wire, write your resignation, and —"

She kissed him. It was not too snappy. Mr. Powell came suddenly from his office. He stopped, wild-eyed. He turned away, a saddened man. He had lost an excellent secretary.

They did not hear him. They were lost in each other's arms, without compass, and didn't care. They belonged together. There were weeks ahead in which to tell each other how and why, and to fit the pieces of the puzzle together. Not many weeks, perhaps, less than they dreamed, thanks to the unspeakable Tojo. But these weeks were theirs and there would be others, afterwards. And meantime.

They spoke in unison. "I love you," they said.

Love, happiness, hope, belief in a mutual future. This is happening now, this will always happen. Nothing can alter it, not war nor rumors of war.

Presently, Tony stood a moment by the door and looked at her.

"That's my girl," he said, in vast content. As he had seen her first, luminous with happiness. But sweetly different. This happiness was his, he had created it. It was a sharper happiness, it had a brighter, keener edge.

It was new; and it would endure.